Balzac's Coffee, DaVinci's Ristorante

Mark Axelrod

VP Festschrift Series:

Volume 1: Christine Brooke-Rose
Volume 2: Gilbert Adair
Volume 3: The Syllabus
Volume 4: Rikki Ducornet
Volume 5: Raymond Federman
(Edited by G.N. Forester and M.J. Nicholls)

Reprint Titles:

The Languages of Love
The Sycamore Tree
The Dear Deceit
The Middlemen
Go When You See the Green Man Walking
Next
Xorandor/Verbivore
by Christine Brooke-Rose

Three Novels — Rosalyn Drexler
Knut — Tom Mallin
Erowina — Tom Mallin
The Greater Infortune/The Connecting Door — Rayner Heppenstall
The Penelope Shuttle Omnibus — Penelope Shuttle
Conversations with Critics — Nicolas Tredell
The Utopian — Michael Westlake
Image for Investigation: About my Father — Christoph Meckel
Meritocrats — Stuart Evans
Bartleby — Chris Scott
How to Outthink a Wall: An Anthology — Marvin Cohen
An Aesthetic of Obscenity: Five Novels — Jeff Nuttall
Imaginary Women — Michael Westlake
A Day at the Office — Robert Alan Jamieson
Caliban's Filibuster — Paul West
The Exagggerations of Peter Prince — Steve Katz
The Alan Burns Omnibus: Volume One — Alan Burns

New fiction:

Mirrors on which dust has fallen — Jeff Bursey

other Verbivoracious titles @
www.verbivoraciouspress.org

Balzac's Coffee,

DaVinci's Ristorante

Mark Axelrod

Verbivoracious Press

Glentrees, 13 Mt Sinai Lane, Singapore

This edition published in Great Britain & Singapore

by Verbivoracious Press

www.verbivoraciouspress.org

ISBN: 978-981-11-3153-0

Printed and bound in Great Britain & Singapore

ACKNOWLEDGEMENTS

I would like to thank Mark Nicholls and Professor Eric Chimenti for all their help in making this book a reality.

DEDICATION

As always, to my son Matías Alejo.

CONTENTS

of restaurants and cafés

of perfumes

Contents

# of hotels and motels

# of businesses miscellaneous

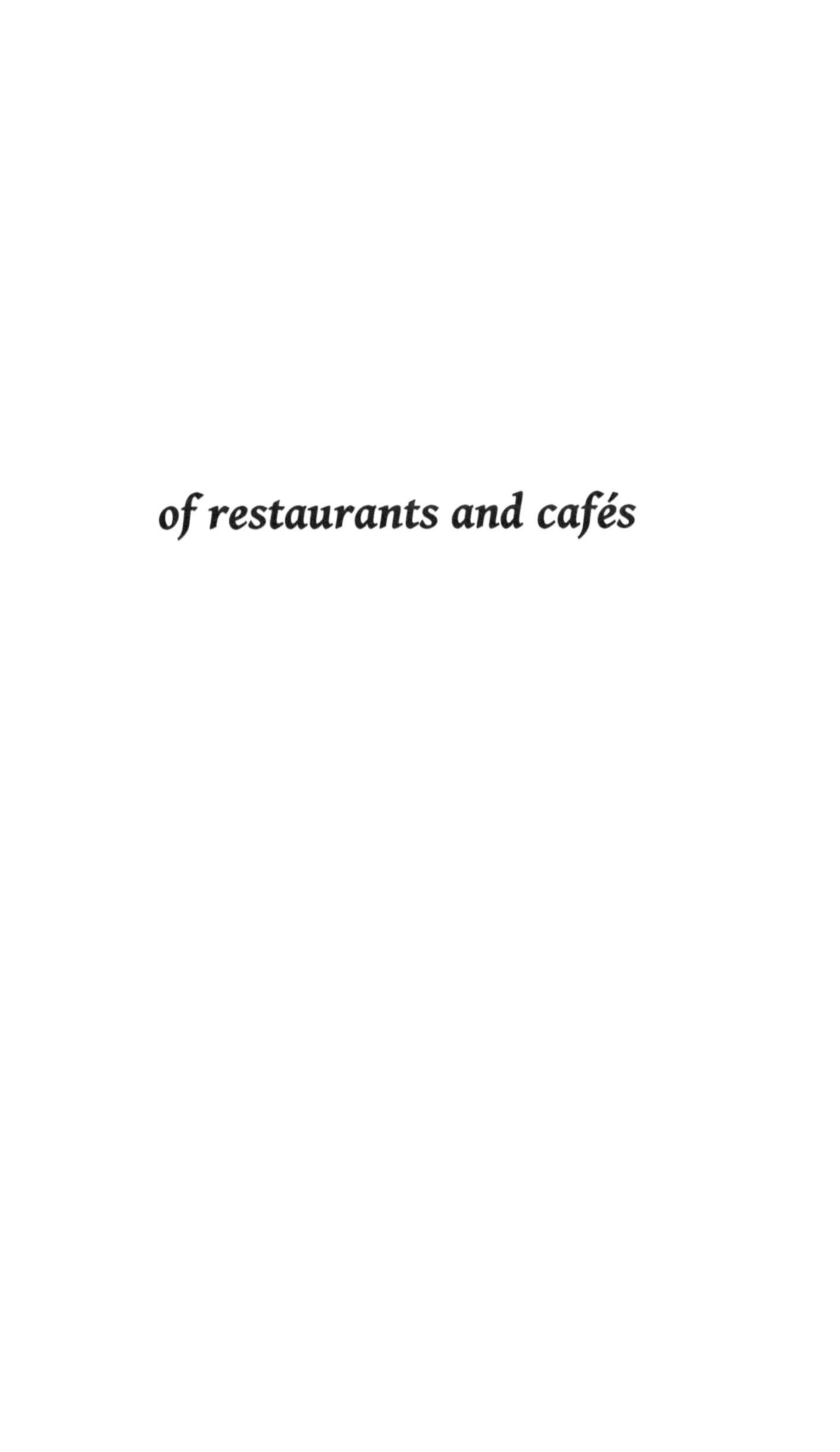

of restaurants and cafés

Balzac Coffee™

Balzac's Coffee™
Hamburg, Germany

"But of course, it's obvious, no?" was Balzac's response to the question posed to him by George Sand during one of the latter's candlelight dinners, "Why a coffee shop?" "Coffee is a great power in my life . . . it chases away sleep, and it gives us the capacity to engage a little longer in the exercise of our intellects," Balzac continued. The fact that Balzac drank an enormous quantity of coffee (Maurois once suggested up to 50 cups per day) would lend credence to the decision. But it wasn't just the stimulation that convinced Balzac, it was something much more tangible. To understand why Balzac went into the business of coffee, one must know what his philosophy of coffee actually was. It's a bit like reading Poe without understanding his *"Philosophy of Composition."* To that end, one needs to read what could be called Balzac's "Philosophy of Caffeine."

"Many people claim that coffee inspires them, but, as everybody knows, coffee only makes boring people more boring. But, as Brillat-Savarin has correctly observed, coffee sets the blood in motion and stimulates the muscles; it accelerates the digestive processes, chases away sleep, and gives us the capacity to engage a little longer in the exercise of our intellects.

Rossini has personally experienced some of these effects as, of course, have I. "Coffee," Rossini told me, "is an affair of fifteen or twenty days; just the right amount of time, fortunately, to write an opera." [After consuming coffee] one wants everything to proceed with the speed of ideas. One actually becomes that fickle character, The Poet, condemned by grocers and their like. One assumes that everyone is equally lucid. A man of spirit must therefore avoid going out in public. Coffee is a great power in my life; I have observed its effects on an epic scale.

For a while . . . you can obtain the right amount of stimulation with one, then two cups of coffee brewed from beans that have been crushed with gradually increasing force and infused with hot water. For another week, by decreasing the amount of water used, by pulverizing the coffee even more finely, and by infusing the grounds with cold water, you can continue to obtain the same cerebral power. When you have produced the finest grind with the least water possible, you double the dose by drinking two cups at a time; particularly vigorous constitutions can tolerate three cups. In this manner, one can continue working for several more days.

Finally, I have discovered a horrible, rather brutal method that I recommend only to men of excessive vigour, men with thick black hair and skin covered with liver spots, men with big square hands and legs shaped like bowling pins. It is a question of using finely pulverized, dense coffee, cold and anhydrous, consumed on an empty stomach. This coffee falls into your stomach, a sack whose velvety interior is lined with tapestries of suckers and papillae. The coffee finds nothing else in the sack, and so it attacks these delicate and voluptuous linings; it acts like a food and demands digestive juices; it wrings and twists the stomach for these juices, appealing as a pythoness appeals to her god; it brutalizes these beautiful stomach linings as a wagon master abuses ponies; the plexus becomes inflamed; sparks shoot all the way up to the brain.

From that moment on, everything becomes agitated. Ideas quick-march into motion like battalions of a grand army to its legendary fighting *ground, and the battle rages. Memories charge in, bright flags on high; the cavalry of metaphor deploys with a magnificent gallop; the artillery of logic rushes up with clattering wagons and cartridges; on imagination's orders, sharpshooters sight and fire; forms and shapes and characters rear up; the paper is spread with ink—for the nightly labour begins and ends with torrents of this black water, as a battle opens and concludes with black powder.*

I recommended this way of drinking coffee to a friend of mine, who absolutely wanted to finish a job promised for the next day: he thought he'd been poisoned and took to his bed, which he guarded like a married man. He was tall, blond, slender and had thinning hair; he apparently had a stomach of papier-mâché. There has been, on my part, a failure of observation.

When you have reached the point of consuming this kind of coffee, then become exhausted and decide that you really must have more, even though you make it of the finest ingredients and take it perfectly fresh, you will fall into horrible sweats, suffer feebleness of the nerves, and undergo episodes of severe drowsiness. I don't know what would happen if you kept at it then: a sensible nature counseled me to stop at this point, seeing that immediate death was not otherwise my fate. To be restored, one must begin with recipes made with milk and chicken and other white meats: finally the tension on the harp strings eases, and one returns to the relaxed, meandering, simple-minded, and cryptogamous life of the retired bourgeoisie.

The state coffee puts one in when it is drunk on an empty stomach under these magisterial conditions produces a kind of animation that looks like anger: one's voice rises, one's gestures suggest unhealthy impatience: one wants everything to proceed with the speed of ideas; one becomes brusque, ill-tempered about nothing. One actually becomes that fickle character, The Poet, condemned by grocers and their like. One assumes that everyone is equally lucid. A man of spirit must therefore avoid going out in public. I discovered this singular state through a series of accidents that made me lose, without any effort, the ecstasy I had been feeling. Some friends, with whom I had gone out to the country, witnessed me arguing about everything, haranguing with monumental bad faith. The following day I recognized my wrongdoing and we searched the cause. My friends were wise men of the first rank, and we found the problem soon enough: coffee wanted its victim. But to be frank, it I had one business I would be eager to engage in, it would be the coffee business. No other would allow me the freedom to express my thoughts without restriction."[1]

So it was that obsession, if not that addiction, plus Balzac's insatiable desire to make a lot of money that drove him to create Balzac's Coffee. However, when it came to business, Balzac was a perpetual failure. He had tried every conceivable scam to make money from publishing fraudulent editions of Molière to starting Balzac's Balls (See: *Borges' Travel, Hemingway's Garage*), but they were all disasters (See: *The Politics of Style in the Fiction of Balzac, Beckett and Cortázar*). However, Balzac was absolutely positive that the coffee business would be his ticket to an early retirement on Antibes and he even said as much to Sand in a note he wrote to her on 31 March 1846: "Coffee shall be my financial elixir just as it has been my creative elixir." Sand, who was a lot better off financially than Balzac, advanced him some money to open the first Balzac's Coffee on the Rue Fortunée on 31 March 1847.

After an initial four months of success, the shop fell on tough times when a harsher than normal winter destroyed a major coffee crop in Colombia and Balzac's manager, a certain Vautrin, absconded with a month's worth of receipts (See *Café Molière*). Balzac became disconsolate. In October 1848, Balzac travelled to the

---

1 *The Reign of Caffeine: Balzac, Coffee, Realism.* François Déconnage. Golden Triangle, N.C.: Dook University Press, 2003.

Ukraine to visit his love, Mme Hanska whose husband had died in 1841. However, neither Madame Hanska's love nor Sand's encouragement nor Chopin's music could comfort him. Disconsolation became depression and depression became dissipation. His health in disrepair, Balzac and Hanska were married in March 1850. Balzac returned with her to Paris, where he tried to salvage what little he could of the business, but died on 18 August 1850.

In order to settle his debts, Balzac's debts, Madame Hanska sold the franchise to a German company which maintains the rights to his name to this day. In death as in life, coffee played a vital role in work. In a letter dated 17 August 1850, Balzac wrote, "if ever a sculpture is chiseled in my memory make sure I am holding a cup of coffee." Rodin was aware of the letter, but thought a cape was more majestic.

Dante's Café

Dante's Café
Amsterdam, NL

Dante was on a roll! After opening a chain of cafés in South America, it was only a matter of time before he opened one in Europe and where else but Amsterdam. But the original idea wasn't Dante's at all. Actually, it was Beatrice Portinari's who suggested the café idea in the first place. In a recently released book by Allesandro Civitas, he writes ". . . the Divine Comedy wasn't meant to be a comedy at all, but a chain of restaurants as witnessed by the café he opened in Santiago de Chile."[2]

Civitas also goes on to say that as early as 10 March 1301, a year to the day before Dante was banished from Florence under pain of death, Beatrice had written Dante with the idea of beginning a restaurant franchise. This new document does shed light on the actual origins of the Dante chain of restaurants. The origin of the South American restaurants has been thoroughly documented (See: *Borges' Travel, Hemingway's Garage*), but how the Amsterdam café originated has long been speculated until Civitas' book.

One has to remember that between his exile in 1302 and the repeal of his sentence in 1315, Dante had spent most of those years in South America. However, according to Civitas, the years 1315-16

---

2 *Alighieri's Appetizers: Dante's La Divina Comida.* Rome: Edizioni Focoso, 2003.

were, until now, undocumented. Some have suggested he was in Romagna, others, Ravenna, but no one had ever suggested Amsterdam. And this is the most astonishing evidence to date. In his research, Civitas discovered that Dante had a long and unknown correspondence and subsequent affair with a 19-year old Dutch milk maiden who only went by the name, Marietje. Just how Dante met Marietje is unknown, but a packet of letters found by Civitas in, of all places, Amsterdam's Red Light District tells the entire story. Known locally as the Walletjes, or generically as Rossebuurt, the district is near two of the city's oldest canals, the Oudezijds Achterburgwal and the Oudezijds Voorburgwal and around the Oudekerkplein, in an area bordered by the Warmoestraat and the Nieuwmarkt. Now just how Civitas "chanced" upon this letter he doesn't say, but the letter has been evaluated and carbon dated and it appears genuine. Unfortunately, the letters Dante sent to Marietje are exact duplicates of those he sent to Beatrice with minor modifications. And though he expresses his love for her in various ways, he is clear in a letter from Ravenna dated 13 August 1321 that his intention was to return to Amsterdam and open a café there with Marietje. Included in the letter was an itinerary and a business plan based on the one he used in Chile and an allusion to the fact that he was not "feeling well" since part of the letter uses the phrase, "pisciare sangue." He was also clear that if anything happened to him, Marietje was to open the café on her own accord. How prescient he was since Dante succumbed only a month later. There is no documentation available on how Marietje found out about Dante's death, though there is some speculation that she became a prostitute and discovered that one of the other women in the brothel had been Dante's consort at one time. Regardless, she followed his directions completely and the café, located at 320 Spuistraat, still stands as a testament to her love for him.

DaVinci's Ristorante

DaVinci's Ristorante
Tustin, California

Ah, DaVinci . . . inventor, military engineer, sculptor, illustrator, architect, scientist, restaurateur. Restaurateur? Yes, it was the DaVinci no one knew about, but it was only a matter of time before DaVinci would open a restaurant since food was so important to him. As a matter of fact, it is now known that the Mona Lisa was actually modeled on a woman who was to become his first waitress![3] It's also patently clear by the subject matter of his paintings: *The Last Supper*, 1497; the *Proportions of the Human Figure*, 1490 (which was originally titled the *Proportions of the Human Waiter*); the restaurant in the background of St. Jerome, 1480; the restaurant in the foreground of the *Annunciation*, originally commissioned for Verrocchio, 1478; the background of the uncompleted, *Adoration of the Magi*, 1482; and the recently discovered sketch books, titled *Coglioneria: Sketches of a Frustrated Restaurateur*. In the sketch book, DaVinci had designed over 236 different restaurants in hopes that some day he might have his own.

This all came to a head 8 April 1476 when Leonardo, then 24, and

---

3 *From Lasagne Magro to Mona Lisa: The Waitress Behind the Genius*, Carlo Emilio Calvino. Milan: Edizioni Scola, 2002.

several others were denounced to the police for having "committed sodomy" with a 17-year old model named Jacopo Saltarelli. The anonymous accusation was found in tamburo outside the Palazzo Vecchio and read that Saltarelli ". . . consents to please those persons who request such wickedness of him" and that he had "served several dozen people." The assumption was that Saltarelli was a male prostitute and though the case came before the courts twice, it was dismissed on both occasions. But the truth was Leonardo and Saltarelli eventually became lovers!

In a recently published book titled *Lui gli ha fatto una bella pipa*[4] it is clear that they had remained lovers for decades and eventually moved to California where, Leonardo thought, homosexuality would be more tolerated. In 1516, a 40-year old Leonardo and a 33-year old Saltarelli, with some funding from Lorenzo di Pietro de' Medici, both sailed to California on board one of Colon's ships, the *La Quaglia* which was headed for the port of San Francisco. Unfortunately, their cartographer became confused and they ended at what is now known as Laguna Beach. What they discovered was a haven for homosexuals and they bought a bungalow there before making their way inland to Tustin where Leonardo fulfilled his desire of opening his own restaurant (and, eventually, a motel) due to the astute real estate savvy of Saltarelli who opened his own real estate agency there as well. But in June, 1518, Leonardo was recalled to Italy to plan the festival at Amboise for the wedding of Lorenzo di Pietro de' Medici and Madeleine de La Tour d'Auvergne. Though he had full intentions of returning to Tustin, that never happened. In January, 1519, he became sick and only a few months later, he died. Hearing of Leonardo's death some months later,

---

4 *Lui gli ha fatto una bella pipa*. Luchresi Rizzarsi. Edizione Foccaccia. Translated by Mark Axelrod as *The Saltarelli Diaries*. Tustin, CA: Saltarelli Press, 2003.

Saltarelli could not face living in Italy without Leonardo and remained in Tustin where he continued to own and operate all three businesses. As living testimony to both of them, the businesses remain to this day.

Eisenstein's Café

Eisenstein's Café
Hamburg, Germany

The question naturally arises: What could be the relationship among Eisenstein, Walter Benjamin, Mickey Mouse and a café in Hamburg bearing the former's name? Well, let's work that one out. There is a very famous photo of Eisenstein shaking hands with Mickey Mouse in 1930 (See: Last Page). What very few people know is that the handshake wasn't done as a publicity stunt, but was actually the conclusion to a business deal that Eisenstein made with the Mouse and brokered by Benjamin to open a café in Hamburg. In her brilliant text, *Hollywood Flatlands: Animation, Critical Theory and the Avant-Garde*, Esther Leslie writes that Walter Benjamin not only mentioned Mickey Mouse in the first draft of his monumental essay, 'The Work of Art in the Age of Mechanical Reproduction', but, at his death, left an assortment of press-cuttings and notes on the Mouse as well.

What Leslie does not include is the chance meeting that took place with Eisenstein, the Mouse and Benjamin at, of all places, Cantor's Delicatessen on Fairfax in July, 1930. In 1929, Eisenstein had arrived in the United States for a tour. He eventually came to Los Angeles where he was befriended by such Hollywood notables as Douglas Fairbanks, von Sternberg, Chaplin, and, eventually,

Disney. But even before he arrived in the United States, Eisenstein had a contractual agreement with Jesse Lasky, who was head of Paramount at the time. Unfortunately, what Eisenstein learned during his tenure in Hollywood was what everyone else knew about the experience and what Brecht was to discover later (See: *Brecht's BMW*).

Though Eisenstein pitched a number of different projects, the Hollywood moguls rejected all of them. And even though two scripts were written, *Sutter's Gold,* about the California gold rush, and *An American Tragedy,* based on Theodore Dreiser's novel, neither project went farther than the script phase. Though Dreiser championed Eisenstein's script, Paramount rejected it flat out. In short, Eisenstein's treatment by the Hollywood moguls was best summed up in a remark attributed to Samuel Goldwyn: "I've seen your film *Potemkin* and admire it very much. What I would like is for you to do something of the same kind, but a little cheaper, for Ronald Coleman."[5] Eisenstein was to have responded to Goldwyn's comment with a comment of his own, "Er zol vaksen vi a stsibeleh, mit dem kop in drerd." The response loses a lot in translation. Back to Cantor's.

Coincidentally, Benjamin happened to be in Los Angeles at the same time conducting a lecture tour that included UCLA. Needing a corned beef fix as Benjamin said, he went to Cantor's where he bumped into Eisenstein. The two were familiar with each other's work and in the course of the conversation Eisenstein mentioned that he was interested in eventually opening a café. Benjamin said that he had some property in Hamburg located adjacent to the Filmstudium at the University of Hamburg and asked if Germany would be okay for him. Eisenstein said, yes.

---

5   Leon Moussinac, *Sergei Eisenstein,* New York: Crown Publishers, 1970, p. 167.

At that very instant, none other than the Mouse walked past their table. Benjamin who knew the Mouse well and had written about him in his essay, immediately invited him to join them whereupon Eisenstein graciously complimented the Mouse on "Steamboat Willie." Eisenstein admired Mickey for being what he called "Plasmatic"—in other words, the Mouse's animated form wasn't fixed, but abstract and flexible like the music that paralleled the script. Embarrassed, the Mouse thanked Eisenstein, asked what he was doing in Los Angeles and soon the conversation returned to the café in Hamburg. Eisenstein said he'd like to open a café in the future as a retirement investment, but really didn't have the capital. That was not a problem for the Mouse who, flush with capital after signing a long-term contract with Disney, suggested the two of them go into partnership and buy Benjamin's property. To make a long story short, the café was opened in 1939, closed during the war, then reopened under new management in 1950. It still operates today adjacent to the Filmstudium at the University of Hamburg where two of its most popular dishes are *Lebkuchen von Mickey* and *Brotzeitteller von Benjamin.*

[The Mouse and Eisenstein sealing the deal at the front door of Cantor's Deli, Fairfax, Los Angeles, California.]

Le Flaubert Salón de Té

Le Flaubert Salón De Té
Santiago, Chile

This was one of those rare coincidences that happened once in a lifetime. Who would have believed there would have been a Franco-Chilean connection between Bouvard and Pécuchet? Extraordinary, but true. But even more extraordinary than that was how it all happened.

It's a well-known fact that Flaubert never finished his novel, *Bouvard and Pécuchet*, before he died. What is little known is how Flaubert planned the ending for the two copyists and what is even less well-known than little-known is what Bouvard and Pécuchet finally did for themselves. Let me clarify.

At his death, Flaubert had only left a plan for the conclusion of the novel, a novel that not only explored all the pettiness of provincial France, but the rather extraordinary lengths Bouvard and Pécuchet went to in order to keep themselves occupied in Chavignolles. From horticulture to chemistry, chemistry to anatomy, anatomy to physiology, physiology to geology, geology to archeology and on and on they studied and yet they were never completely satisfied with what they had learned or accomplished.

Dissatisfied with everything that Flaubert had written for them, the two characters took it upon themselves to do something radical.

Separating themselves from the pages of the novel (no mean feat in and of itself) they began to study the art of gastronomy, the science of the cuisine. They began with sauces, moved on to soups, from there to entrées and eggs, poultry and game, meat and fish, potatoes, rice and pasta, then on to vegetables and salads, and, finally, to desserts and pastry and wine.

They fashioned menus that became known throughout France. Their most famous, known simply as *Le Bovary*, included soups of *Consommé Printanier* and *Bisque d'écrevisses*; removes of *Turbot sauce aux huîtres* and *Filet de Boeuf à la Richelieu*; entrées of *Timbales au Salpicon* or *Foies de canard à la Toulousaine* or *Chaud-froid de gibier à l'écarlate*; roasts like *Dinde truffé franquée d'ortolans* and *Faisans rôtis*; side dishes of *Petits pois à la Française* and *Cardons à la moëlle*; and desserts like *Petits soufflés glacés à l'ananas* and *Gateau moka à la Parisienne*. But the one dish that became their specialty known throughout France from Chavignolles to Paris, Marseilles to Yonville, Rouen to Tostes, was their *Bouilleture d'anguilles à l'angevine*. Curiously, after several years of incredible financial and critical success, Bouvard and Pécuchet decided that the provincial Chavignolles had had enough of their superior cuisine and keeping with their collective behavior of obsessive agitation, they pondered a move.

"Do you think we should?" asked Pécuchet

"Might it be worth a try?" answered Bouvard.

"What dish?"

"What course?"

"The potage?

"The relevés?"

"The rotîs?"

"The entrées?"

All of those ideas and many others ran rampant through the

collective mind of Bouvard and Pécuchet until they chanced upon an idea that astonished them both. An idea that arrived at their collective mind simultaneously.

"Poisson!!!!!!!!!!"

"But where?" they thought.

"Calais? Cassis? Antibes?"

"No, no, somewhere out of this world!" exclaimed Bouvard.

"Somewhere exotic!" shouted Pécuchet.

"A city near a coast!" added Bouvard.

"They must have eels."

"Which must have sauce."

They looked at each other and raised their eyebrows simultaneously.

"Santiago!!!!!!!!!!!" they exclaimed in unison.

And so the journey began from Chavignolles to Calais, Calais to Buenos Aires, Buenos Aires to Mendoza, Mendoza to Santiago de Chile where they finally settled in the *commun* of Providencia and opened their café at Orrego Luco, 125 between the Avda. Andres Bello and Avda. Providencia. And to honor their *maestro*, the man who gave them life and who was fond of all things Epicurian, they named the café, *Le Flaubert*. Nothing would have made their master happier. On the evening before we left Santiago we ate there. The *congrio margarita* would have made the *maestro* proud.

Goya's Café

Goya's Café
Buenos Aires, Argentina

It was irony indeed that led Goya from Spain to Argentina and even more ironic to think of how his life ended. It all began in the winter of 1792 when Goya contracted lung infection while on a visit to the tiny fishing village of Nerja on the Costa del Sol. It impaired his breathing and marked a turning point in his career as a more lugubrious mood entered his work. Between 1797 and 1799, he drew and etched the first of his great print series The Caprices, which not only mocked Spanish manners, but their superstitions as well. The next two decades produced *Disasters of War*, 1810 and *Absurdities*, 1820-1823, which were scathing testimonials on the human condition. The horrors of war and the concomitant abuses of human rights were of primary concern to Goya who witnessed the massacre of Spanish citizens during Napoleon's occupation of Spain. In 1814 he completed the *Second of May, 1808* and *Third of May, 1808* both of which detail the brutality of the French against unarmed peasants. Little was Goya to know that he would later suffer the same brutal end. Eventually, the oppressive political situation in Spain forced him to depart for France in 1824 and too was a turning point in Goya's life.

Late in November of that year, Goya met the then 22-year old

Victor Hugo who was working on the manuscript of *Notre-Dame de Paris* that would be published only seven years later. It was an extraordinary set of circumstances which Hugo vividly recounts in one of his journals[6] in which Hugo was sitting by himself at the Procope when in walked the 78-year old Goya assisted by two friends. Hugo was familiar with Goya's paintings, especially The Caprices, yet seeing the master face to face was too good for Hugo to believe and he wasn't sure what to do. He wanted desperately to approach the maestro and tell him how much he admired his work, but felt absolutely intimidated by the Hispanic giant. Eventually, however, Hugo garnered enough courage to walk to his table and introduce himself and the four of them sat down for a marvelous discussion about politics, the occult, and human folly. Hugo could tell that Goya was not well since "he coughed incessantly" and asked him if he had plans to remain in France. Goya said he would be moving to Bordeaux soon, but it was Hugo who suggested that, perhaps, somewhere else, where the air was fresher, would be better for his health. As a way of accenting that, Hugo unconsciously blurted out, "buenos aires," then corrected himself in French. But Goya immediately lit up when he heard the words and turned to his compatriots and repeated, "Mi Buenos Aires querido."

It was only a matter of time before Goya was on his way to Argentina and once ensconced he decided to open a café with artwork on walls and coffee in goblets. He was so enthusiastic about the idea that he brought *The Third of May* with him and hung it on a wall opposite *The Burial of the Sardine*. It didn't bother him that the Café Tortoni was down the street since he knew artists from all over the city would come and frequent his café. What he didn't

---

6 *Burial of the Sardine and Other Fish.* Victor Hugo. Paris: Charpentier, 1880.

count on was the horror of what was to follow.

Two of Goya's most frequent customers were young painters: Dario Santillan and Maximiliano Kosteki, both of whom were also known as political protestors. That reputation didn't bother Goya who was a political protestor himself. What changed everything was when Goya discovered that both young men were summarily executed by the Argentine police during the "Dirty Little War." Subsequent to their murders, the police then came to Goya's café looking for him. The man in charge was Ricardo Miguel Cavallo and alleged interrogator at a clandestine torture center based at the School of Naval Mechanics, known as ESMA. What happened next is well-documented. Because Cavallo was the also the captain of a frigate, he had Goya and about a dozen other alleged taken ESMA where they were interrogated for hours before they were thrown on board the ship Esmeralda Dos and taken out to sea somewhere off the Mar del Plata. Once there, Cavallo thought it amusing to re-stage Goya's *The Shootings of May Third 1808* complete with six executioners dressed in Napoleonic uniforms. Goya, hands outstretched, was in the middle. After the men were executed, their bodies were pushed overboard. Ironically, it was a French ship that found Goya's body floating in the Atlantic and returned it to Bordeaux where he was buried. And the café? It still remains on the Avenida de Mayo as a testimony to living and the dead.

Hemingway's Café

Hemingway's Café
Laguna Beach, California

Buoyed by the success of the garage (See: *Borges' Travel, Hemingway's Garage*), Hemingway decided to expand into the always profitable café business and chose Laguna Beach as the best place to do that. He decided to do that after visiting and seeing the Victor Hugo Inn located near the sloping, geranium-covered banks of Heisler Park that overlooked the Pacific in Laguna Beach, California. His immediate response to seeing the inn was, "If that fucking no talent frog can open up a successful restaurant, then so can I!"[7] First he looked for the perfect location which he found on Forest Avenue in Laguna Beach. It was a clean, well-lighted place, intimate, with few tables, it allowed everyone in the restaurant to hear him when he talked which was one of the reasons he wanted to open the restaurant in the first place. Then he set out to find the best chef he could find for the least amount of money and recruited Jean-Francois Perrier whom he had met while in Paris. The two of them decided on a menu which was more to Hemingway's liking than to Perrier's, but they came up with a menu that sported such Hemingway favorites as: *Salade Torrents of Spring* (a recipe that he

---

7   *Hemingway's Piquant Journals.* Edited by Scott Fitzgerald. Oak Park, IL: In Your Face Press, 1948.

stole from Turgenev); *Ernie's Cold Cucumber Soup*; *Paella de Nerja*; *Fillet of Lioness*; the ever popular, *Pipe du Tigre*; *Big Game Hunter's Safari Sirloin*; *Canary for One*; *Old Man and the Sea Souffle*; *A Moveable Feast* (for 2) and, of course, *Hills Like White Elephant Stew*.

For entertainment, Hemingway would usually read from his own works (since he couldn't stand anyone else's) and, on occasion, he'd engage in some stand-up comedy. His stand-up routine generally included ethnic jokes about people he knew and his favorite routines were about Jews and homosexuals. Obviously, when Hemingway decided to open his restaurant in Laguna Beach he didn't really make a demographic study of his patrons or else he might not have been so caustic. At any rate, his penchant for discrimination all came to head one night when he started in on Dorothy Parker.

"But seriously ladies and gentlemen," Hemingway began, *"let me tell you something about Dorothy Parker. Now there was a woman who was really fucked up. How fucked up? Listen to this poem I wrote about her and you decide . . .*

> *'O thou who with a safety razor blade*
> *a new one to avoid infection*
> *Slit both thy wrists*
> *the scars defy detection*
> *Who over-veronaled to try and peek*
> *into the shade*
> *Of that undistant country from whose bourne*
> *no traveler returns who hasn't been there.*
> *But always vomited in time*
> *and bound your wrists up*
> *To tell how you could see his little hands*
> *already formed*

You'd waited months too long
that was the trouble.
But you loved dogs and other people's children
and hated Spain where they are cruel to donkeys.
Hoping the bulls would kill the matadors.
The national tune of Spain was Tea for Two
you said and don't let anyone say pain to you—
You'd seen it with the Seldes
One Jew, his wife and a consumptive
you sneered your way around
through Aragon, Castille and Andalucia.
Spaniards pinched
the Jewish cheeks of your plump ass
in holy week in Seville.
forgetful of our Lord and of His passion.
Returned, your ass intact, to Paris
To write more poems for the New Yorker.'

Pretty fucked up, eh?"

But if that weren't bad enough, he then started in on gaybashing and before one could say *Sodome et Gomorrhe*, the place was empty except for A.E. Hotchner who sat by himself shaking his head and nursing his drink. It didn't take long for the word to get around the gay community in Laguna Beach and before long the café closed; however, in a fit of pique, Hemingway bought the property and kept the sign outside as a reminder to everyone in Laguna Beach just how important he actually was.

Molière Café

Molière's Café
Buenos Aires, Argentina

Just where the exact idea came from is open to speculation, but a recent book on Louis XIV titled *"Secret Conversations: Molière Meets Louis XIV,"* may help explain it. It is common knowledge that on the evening of 24 October 24 1658, Molière and his troupe performed for the first time before Louis XIV and his courtiers in the Guard Room of the old Louvre Palace. It is also common knowledge that instead of performing Cornielle's *Nicoméde*, they performed one of their popular farces. This gaffe could have resulted in dramatically tragic results until Molière apologized to the King and suggested they perform his own play, *The Love-Sick Doctor*. Even Molière had no idea what would happen next. The King complied, the play was a critical success and Molière's company (which henceforth would be called the *Troupe de Monsieur*) was afforded the use of the Hôtel du Petit Bourbon, one of the three most important theaters in Paris at the time.

Everything seemed to going Molière's way. He had his own company, his own venue and the freedom to perform whatever he wished to perform. The first play to be staged there was *Les Précieuses Ridicules* or *The Pretentious Ladies*. Incredibly successful, the King rewarded Molière with a handsome grant and though, for political reasons, the troupe finally had to move from the Petit Bourbon to the Théâtre du Palais Royal, Molière was quite content with the direction of his career. And though the troupe eventually became so popular that it was even called the "Troupe of the King" there were problems with the management of the theatre. Specifically, the concessions.

It seems as if the theatre patrons at the time were not disinclined to want something to eat or drink in between acts. This was something not in fashion at the time. That is, one attended the theatre just to do that: attend. No one actually expected to eat there though the word reached the King that some people were actually leaving the theatre early because of "hunger pains." Always perspicacious, the King suggested to Molière that, perhaps, a beverage or a snack midway in the performance might be something that would mitigate the early departure of the patrons. Molière considered the idea and suggested to his wife and actress, Madeleine Béjart,[8] that she hire some people to run the concession stand at the theatre. What no one knows is that the person Béjart hired to run the concession stand was a an ex-actor by the name of Jean-Daniel Rattuffe and what transpired is a bit of theatrical history that has gone relatively unnoticed for over three centuries.

What we've been able to discover about Rattuffe is that he was hired by Molière because of his ability to deal with people effectively. Molière trusted Rattuffe to buy the food and beverages and to serve the theatre clientele respectfully and with cordiality. Hired in 1660, Rattuffe worked for Molière for the next four years until it was discovered that he had been embezzling funds from the

---

8 Some believe that because of the 20 year difference between Molière and Béjart that, perhaps, she was something more than his wife, but his daughter from an illicit love affair. Recent DNA testing has not conclusively proven this.

concession coffers for that entire time.[9] It was only in 1663 that the scam was discovered though the money wasn't. Incensed, Molière went to the King to gain some kind of aid to convict Rattuffe of his crimes. The King obliged and Rattuffe was sent to prison. This tale of misbegotten wealth was, of course, the genesis of one of Molière's most famous plays, *Tartuffe, the Hypocrite* the first three acts of which were presented at Versailles on 12 May 1664. But what happened to the money?

Curiously, almost a decade to the day after Rattuffe was convicted, a strong box filled with cash was mysteriously left at the box office of the Théâtre du Palais Royal with a note that merely said all the money was accounted for. Just how the money got there was and still is a mystery though some suggest that Rattuffe had a family in Paris and for ten years they invested the money in mutual funds before taking the profits and returning the principal without interest. Regardless, Molière took the money and decided that, upon retirement, he and Béjart would open a café in Buenos Aires since it was suggested the "good air" of Argentina would be helpful in reducing Molière's constant migraine headaches.

Unfortunately, that's not what happened. On 17 February 1673, Molière suffered a hemorrhage while playing the role of the hypochondriac, Argan in *The Imaginary Invalid*. And though he died later that night, his last words to Béjart were, "Do as we planned and I shall always be with you in the city of good air." She did as he had bid her and the café remains today in Buenos Aires.

---

9   *From Rattuffe to Tartuffe: The Mask of Marginality.* Orgon Goinfre. Charenton: Maison de Fous, 2003.

Mozart's Café

Mozart's Café
New York City, NY

Oh, there has been a lot of speculation about what actually killed Mozart. It has been suggested that because Mozart allegedly suffered from rheumatic fever as a child scientists have opened the possibility of the disease damaging his heart and then later in his life being the cause of his death. This theory sounds plausible based on the rash and the fever for rheumatic fever and the swollen limbs which point to a commonly known byproduct of heart failure. Others have suggested that his death was due to poisoning, still others, renal failure.

Perhaps no other composer has had so many legends develop surrounding their death. The composer Antonio Salieri, in a deathbed confession, tried to take credit for murdering Mozart. There was a popular rumor that Mozart's Masonic Lodge had assassinated him for betraying lodge secrets in his opera "Die Zauberflute", but this has never been proven. In 1901, a skull, whose "discoverers" contested was Mozart's was donated to the Salzburg Mozarteum. Legend has it that Mozart's gravedigger, Joseph Rothmayer, allegedly retrieved the skull before the bones were pulverized in a recycling program (i.e. so the burial plot could be reused) in 1801. Just how Joseph Rothmayer could have detected that it was Mozart's skull (since Mozart was dumped into unmarked grave) has never been scrutinized. Forensic examination of the skull was inconclusive except for the fact that whomever belonged to the skull died of chronic haematoma possibly resulting from a fall. The Mozarteum has not accepted the findings of the French team and has been conducting its own studies. For further information see "Archeology"—March/April 1991: "*The Mystery of Mozart's Skull*" and the book *After the Funeral: The Posthumous Adventures of Famous Corpses* by Edwin A. Murphy. Since that conclusion was inconclusive, the cause of death was attributed to Miliary Fever or tuberculosis throughout the body that affects the bones and joints, or the brain. So what's it gonna be, eh?

Well, the truth is stranger than fiction. It's common knowledge that Mozart's fame began to wane after "*Le nozze di Figaro*", 1785 and he sank deeper into debt and depression as well as finding himself hungry. This hunger began to manifest itself in his composing as well and beginning in 1791 one can see just how pervasive his "hunger" compositions became: Song with Piano, "*Komm, das Essen*"; Song with Piano, "*Die Speise*"; the Cantata, "*Der Ernährungsminister*"; the Opera, "*Die Lebensmittelknappheit*"; the Opera, seria, "*Der Hungerlohn*"; the Cantata, "*Vor Hunger Sterben*"; the comic duet, "*Am Arsch der Welt*"; and, finally, the Requiem Mass which was originally titled, "*Den Arsch Hängen Lassen.*" When all seemed lost, he found succorance with a fellow Freemason, Michael Puchberg. Mozart had joined the Masons in 1784 and remained one until his death. Puchberg was a native New Yorker and had connections with the restaurant business in Manhattan.

Puchberg asked Mozart what he thought of going into the restaurant business and the latter, starving both literally and metaphorically, jumped at the chance. Puchberg told Mozart that he and his cousin needed a third partner to open a restaurant in

New York and Amadeus was thrilled with the idea. Puchberg booked Mozart passage on board the ship Esmeralda (this was an unfortunate choice of ships since the *Esmeralda* was also the name of the ship von Aschenbach sailed on in Visconti's, *Death in Venice*; of course, Mozart didn't know that at the time) and sailed into New York harbor on 22 November 1791. No sooner had he got there when Puchberg's cousin, Rudy, whisked Mozart off to the café on West 70th Street. At the time, the café was in the final stages of decoration and that night it would have been a kind of rehearsal dinner. Mozart was thrilled and was actually in the kitchen whipping up Austrian delicacies such as pear salad with Raspberry Vinegar, Tafelspitz with Apfelkren and Mohr im Hemd. What happened next one could only describe as fatal. Somehow the Tafelspitz was not prepared properly. This has been a point of speculation for many years, but finally came out in a book written by the Austrian food scholar, Kurt Waldeneggar.[10] In the book, Waldeneggar traces what happened subsequent to the rehearsal dinner.

Later that night, Mozart began experiencing a number of symptoms including vomiting, nausea, a low-grade fever, abdominal cramps and diarrhea all classical signs of *E coli* poisoning; however, the physicians couldn't diagnose the problem very effectively. All Mozart wanted to do at that time, was return home and so Rudy put him back on the Esmeralda and sent him back to Vienna. It was on board the Esmeralda that Mozart began the *Requiem "Den Arsch Hängen Lassen."* By the time Mozart got home, the disease was rampant and on 5 December, 1791, he died. Since he was connected to Puchberg and Puchberg's cousin, Rudy, it

---

10 *From Raw to Requiem: E Coli and the Death of Mozart*. Kurt Waldeneggar. Berlin: Scheissbolle Verlag, 2003.

led to the false rumors of some nefarious poisoning, though it was clearly due to the ill-prepared Tafelspitz.

Mozart, of course, was buried in an unmarked grave at the cemetery of Saint Marx, a Viennese suburb. In homage to the maestro, and feeling as if he were somehow responsible for his death, Rudy changed the name of the café from Puchberg's to Mozart's where it still remains to this day at 140 W. 70th Street where Mohr im Hemd is still the dessert specialty of the house.

Pascal's Café

Pascal's Café
Costa Mesa, California

While Montaigne dealt with skepticism with a certain kind of Gallic bravura, Pascal was tormented by religious doubt. This obsession often revolved around the question: "Why are we here?" to which Pascal, with cogent philosophical acumen, attempted to answer in his book, *Pensées*. But what has only come to light recently was that the book, *Pensées*, was not the *first book* he wrote on that subject, but the *second!* The first book, newly discovered and translated was titled, *Pensées du Cusine* (translated as *Thoughts from the Kitchen*).[11] This brilliant discovery casts new light on many of Pascal's theories.

Pascal once wrote, "The eternal silence of these infinite spaces terrifies me." For centuries it's been thought that for Pascal the universe was devoid of meaning without Christianity. As T.S. Eliot, once wrote, "Pascal's disillusioned analysis of human bondage is sometimes interpreted to mean that Pascal was really and finally an unbeliever, who, in his despair, was incapable of enduring reality and enjoying the heroic satisfaction of the free man's worship of nothing. His despair, his disillusion, are, however, no

---

11 *Thoughts from the Kitchen*, translated by Mark Axelrod. Los Angeles: Green Integer Press, 2003.

illustration of personal weakness; they are perfectly objective, because they are essential moments in the progress of the intellectual soul; and for the type of Pascal they are the analogue of the drought, the dark night, which is an essential stage in the progress of the Christian mystic."[12] But what Eliot failed to include was the fact that Pascal found meaning in the universe in the unlikeliest of places: the kitchen.

It is common knowledge that Pascal conceded belief in God could only be a matter of personal choice. This "speculative approach" to the existence of God is seen in the vast majority of Pascal's works, but it is only in his *Kitchen Thoughts* that the true nature of the Pascal's belief in the universe comes to fruition. But the real reason for such a radical change in his attitude can be found in a mystical experience he had. On 23 November 1654, Pascal was returning from town after buying some bread. He was driving a four-in-hand when the horses, suddenly spooked, took off; the two lead horses dashed over the parapet of the bridge at Neuilly, and Pascal was saved only by the loaves of bread that actually softened his fall. Always somewhat of a mystic, Pascal considered this a special summons to abandon the world and he wrote the following account of the accident on a small piece of parchment: "I have discovered the baking of bread is tantamount to the origin of the universe and that every loaf is a recapitulation of God's majestic creation. No other loaf reaffirms that creation better than the bâtard. It is for that reason that I shall devote my future studies to the perfection of that doughy art." Not long after that religious experience, he pledged his life to baking and la cuisine. What happened next is extraordinary.

Pascal made a visit to the Jansenist monastery Port-Royal des

---

12 *Selected Essays on Cooking*, T.S. Eliot. London: Shagitz Press, 1964.

Champs about twenty miles southwest of Paris. Once there, he discovered, to his fascination, a Native American Indian of the Esselen tribe of Monterey, California who went by the name of Olivalla. The Esselen lived in the upper Carmel Valley, in the rugged and densely-forested Santa Lucia Mountains, now a part of the Los Padres National Forest. Needless to say, he was fascinated by Olivalla who, along with most of his tribe, were forced off their native lands by the United States government. What Pascal learned from Olivalla was how to bake, but more important, it was Olivalla who suggested he visit Tassajara, a Zen Buddhist community whose hot springs were used by Esselen Indians and whose meals were known throughout the world. Pascal did exactly what Olivalla suggested and on 31 March 1660, he left Calais for Monterey and, eventually, Tassajara at which point he began to create an entirely different kind of cooking: Franco-Tassajaran. But the journey doesn't stop there.

After a year at Tassajara, Pascal happened to having brunch in Carmel, when he chanced upon a copy of *Gourmet Magazine* that listed a restaurant for sale in Costa Mesa, California. He felt that discovery was his destiny and he immediately contacted the person interested in selling the café. To make a long story a short story, Pascal bought the restaurant in Costa Mesa and had a grand opening on 31 March 1661. Unfortunately, family problems forced him to return to Paris. Always of fragile constitution, he took sick and died 19 August 1662 of what some believe to have been stomach ulcers. The truth was found sewn in his clothing on his death. It was a note that said how much he missed the café and that bread would always be his salvation. Ironically, it would have been sourdough bread that might have saved his life. The café which was originally located in the South Coast Shopping Center, Costa Mesa, California, has since relocated to Newport Beach.

Rembrandt's Café

Café Rembrandt
Amsterdam, NL

Everyone knows about Rembrandt's success with toothpaste (See: *Borges' Travel, Hemingway's Garage*), but not everyone knows about the failure he had with the café business since the origins of the café are not that well documented. But it should have come as no surprise that Rembrandt would have tried his hand at the café business given the penchant he had for painting cafés. We can see that in such paintings as: *The Shooting Company of Captain Frans Banning Cocq at a Café* (1642, Rijksmuseum); *Portrait of the Painter in Old Age at a Café* (1669? National Gallery, London); *Potiphar's Wife Accusing Joseph at a Café* (1655, Staatliche Museen, Berlin-Dahlem); and *Return of the Prodigal Son from a Café* (1669?, the Hermitage). It can also be seen in his graphic work such as, *The Finding of Moses at a Café* (1635? Rijksprentenkabinet, Amsterdam); *The Eastern Café at Rhenen* (Oostpoort) (1648? Musée, Bayonne, France); *Portrait of a Man in an Armchair at a Café, Seen Through a Frame* (1634, private collection, New York City); and *A Woman Sleeping in a Café* (Hendrickje?) (1655? British Museum, London). Likewise, many of his famous etchings have the café as a background such as, *Christ Healing the Sick at a Café*, also known as the 200 Guilder Print (1642-1645?); the poetic cityscape, *Three Cafés*

(1643); and, lastly, *Christ Preaching at a Café* (1652?), all of which are in the British Museum.

It's common knowledge as well that Rembrandt had to declare bankruptcy in 1656 to pay his debts. Unfortunately, the results of the auction-including the sale of his house were disappointing and he clearly had to find another source of income. Enter Matthijs Afzetter. Matthijs Afzetter was a well-known Amsterdam jeweler who, as is now known, was the subject in Rembrandt's *Old Man with a Gold Chain* (Oil on panel, c. 1631) which Rembrandt did in exchange for some jewelry he gave to his wife. But 25 years later, jewelry was the last thing on Rembrandt's mind, when Afzetter showed up at the auction. Witnessing Rembrandt's plight, Afzetter suggested the two of them go out to Rembrandt's favorite café, the Café Verzinsel, in order to talk business. The business Afzetter suggested was simple: he knew Rembrandt loved that particular café and would advance him the money to buy the café in exchange for any two paintings of his choice. Realizing that such a deal would get him out of debt and offer him a comfortable retirement, Rembrandt agreed and the deal was consummated in early 1657, but it wasn't for another eight years before Afzetter called in the agreement. Afzetter, who was Jewish, commissioned Rembrandt to do a painting of he and his new wife, which is the well-known *Jewish Bride* (c. 1665, Oil on canvas, Rijksmuseum, Amsterdam), then chose Rembrandt's *Self-Portrait* (c.1658 Oil on canvas) to close the deal.

Upon Rembrandt's death in 1669, the café fell into disrepair and was eventually taken over by Afzetter's son. After changing many hands and many venues, the café finally ended up at the most unlikely of places, Amsterdam's Schiphol Airport where you can drink an Oranjeboom Lager today.

Van Gogh's Brasserie

Van Gogh's Brasserie
Amsterdam, NL

It was a natural transition. Though little is known about Van Gogh's attempts at selling potatoes in Helsinki, Finland (which, of course, was the genesis for his *The Potato Eaters*) [See: *Borges' Travel, Hemingway's Garage*] what's even less known about him was his brief tenure in Paris (1886-1888) where he lived with his brother, Theo, at 54 rue Lepic in Paris's Montmartre district. For Vincent, the time was well spent in Paris where he occasioned the exhibitions of the Impressionists like Degas, Monet, Renoir, Pissarro, and Seurat among others. Little is known about his time in Paris since most of what occurred has been gleaned from the letters written between he and Theo, but what is patently evident is that one cannot live in France without being affected by café life. And Vincent was not immune. This is evident in a letter Vincent wrote to Theo while living in Arles. Van Gogh moved to Arles in early 1888 seeking the warmth of Provence. Unfortunately, Vincent met not with the sunshine he expected, but with a combination of finger numbing cold weather and the "Mistral," the blustery winds that swoop down the Rhone Valley and blow into Provence as a gust from the west. The Mistral could last for days and it often precluded Vincent from attempting any painting whatsoever. At those times, he would retreat to the cafés and the café that inspired him most was the one which became the model for the painting *Le Café-Le Soir*, Vergessieu's Brasserie in Cassis. In a letter dated February 24, 1888, Van Gogh writes about his interest in cafés:

> *My dear Theo, though I have not been here long, I have been here long enough to shiver from the winds of the Mistral. Their howling unnerves me and almost makes me long for the warmth of a Paris café. I have sought out such a place here and found one to my liking. The owner, Monsieur Vergessieu, is very charming and allows me time enough to sketch and to write letters. He often refills my coffee at no charge since he must know that I have but little money to spend on such extravagances. He occasionally gives me food that he suggests would go to waste if I did not eat it. I have asked to paint his portrait in exchange for his kindness and he has agreed. I have often thought how wonderful it would be to have my own café. A café where writers and painters could come and sort out their thoughts, their dreams, their visions of better futures and moribund pasts. I have thought that, perhaps, you and I, dear brother, could do that together and I envision a day when, working side by side, we might have our own brasserie. When you have the time, might you be able to send me some cerulean blue? I am at the end of what little I have. With a good hand shake, Vincent.*[13]

Little did he know that his dream would become a reality, when

---

13 *Vincent & Me*. Marcel Vergesseieu. Translated from the French by Marten Asroede. Amsterdam: Boekenwereld, N.L., 1902.

Van Gogh's Uncle Vincent died and left a legacy to Theo. This financial windfall not only enabled Theo to sponsor Gauguin's move to Arles, but also became the down payment for the café that Vincent had alluded to since Theo had returned to Amsterdam and parlayed some of that money into establishing what would become known as, *Van Gogh's Brasserie.*

The irony, of course, was that as Theo was dutifully working on the business of making the café a reality, Vincent's continued malnutrition slowly contributed to his declining health. Who's to say whether a better diet might have prolonged Van Gogh's life? Clearly, there may have been a link between his mental state and his lack of nutrition. But regardless of what effect diet may or may not have played in Van Gogh's last months of life, he died on 29 July 1890 and Theo died six months later. As an homage to both her husband and her brother-in-law, Theo's wife, Johanna, took it upon herself to resume Vincent's dream of having a café of his own and opened the brasserie in 1893. Still active, alive and always receptive to artists, Van Gogh's Brasserie celebrated its centenary in 2003.

Café Mahler

Café Mahler
Buenos Aires, Argentina

Mahler had a heart condition. Mitral valve prolapse. Actually, it was, and is, quite a benign heart condition though it is linked to a confusing array of seemingly unrelated symptoms, from shortness of breath to panic attacks. Mitral valve prolapse is generally the most benign of the various types of heart murmurs, and is probably genetic in origin. Mitral valve prolapse is named for a heart valve and is usually first diagnosed as a faint heart "click" or murmur, though it isn't a form of "heart disease" in any substantial way. But Mahler, sensitive to music as well as physiology, must have sensed that "click" even before it was diagnosed since, if one listens closely, one can hear the "click" in all of his symphonies prior to his famous *Sixth*. But one has to return to the night of 27 May 1906, in Essen to see where all of this began.

Mahler wrote his Sixth symphony between 1903 and 1905, a time that, arguably, was one of the most productive and least agitated in his life. Though his previous symphonies registered triumph (1, 2, 5, 7 and 8), serenity (3, 4) or resignation (*Das Lied*, 9 and 10) the sixth is his most lugubrious. What makes it his most lugubrious are the hammer strikes. Now what people don't know about Mahler was that he was a perfervid reader of Jewish mysticism and his favorite work was the Kabbalah. But he was also a perfervid tarot card reader and on that particular May evening, prior to the performance, he read his own cards. What resulted was clearly prescient for the cards dictated that 3 things would happen to him subsequent to the performance.[14] Mahler looked upon that reading as the "three blows of fate" which befell the hero of his symphony and which were achieved by three hammer blows heard at the finale of the piece; however, historically the same three blows have been viewed as the three blows that befell Mahler in 1907 with the death of his daughter, Putzi, who died of scarlet fever (which also tended to debilitate the heart muscle); his own diagnosis of mitral valve prolapse; and his subsequent resignation from his position as director of the Vienna *Hofoper*. Clearly, these three blows were instrumental in rearranging his life. But what happened subsequent to his diagnosis is fascinating.

Mahler, despondent over his recent spate of difficulties, returned to a reading of the Tarot. The cards were mysterious, but seemed to imply that a change of venue was forthcoming and he received an offer to conduct the Metropolitan Opera. Two years later, he accepted a post with the New York Philharmonic, but Mahler's time in New York wasn't the best. Only 50 in 1910, Mahler began thinking of retirement. While nursing a café in Soho, Mahler saw a copy of *El Pais* on an adjacent table. He picked up the paper and began perusing the pages when he chanced upon an ad that offered a café for sale in Buenos Aires a city that was second only to New York in its Jewish population and a city that, for Mahler, seemed to be replete with a kind of energy that he needed to reinvigorate himself. After discussing the possibility with Alma, his wife, the two

---

14 *From Alchemy to the Zohar: Mahler's Mysterious Mantras.* Teddy Adorno. Berlin: Weltschmerz Verlag, 2003.

left New York on 4 July 1910 for a cruise to Argentina. Though little is known of what transpired on the cruise, what is known is that Mahler invested in the café presumably with the understanding that he would return after his tenure with the Philharmonic was over. Alas, that wasn't to be and on 18 May 1911 Mahler died, not of the heart disease he feared most, but of viral streptococcus; however, the café remains and serves a Café Das Lied in his memory.

J.S. Bach's Sonata™

J.S. Bach's Sonata™
Leipzig, Germany

The incidents leading up to Bach's entry in the perfume business are as extraordinary as a life in which over a thousand compositions were written. It all began with his first wife, his cousin Maria Barbara Bach. Though she tried every means to get pregnant, all attempts proved fruitless since Bach couldn't get it up. Apparently, the maestro's energies were consumed by composing and his sexual proclivities were negligible. By sheer accident, Bach was composing one of his most mellifluous sonatas for flute and recorder (known later as the famous, Ständer Sonata) when he accidentally knocked over a scented candle. The melted wax oozed over the papers. Agitated, Bach quickly tried to clean up the mess, but found himself enchanted with the scent. So enchanted that he got an erection.

Obsessed with his newly found discovery, he went to a chemist friend of his, Herr Wolfgang Stecher, and asked him if he could make a perfume from the scent and that was easily done. At least seven times he had his wife use the perfume and she bore him seven children until she died in 1720. A year later, he married Anna Magdalena Wülken, but to make sure the perfume wasn't a fluke, he used it on her and eventually she bore him 13 children. Realizing the perfume had extraordinary aphrodisiacal qualities, he moved his family to Leipzig where he became the musical director of the church of St. Thomas and continued to produce, Sonata, his most famous contribution to the world of music and procreation.

Puccini's Bohème™

Puccini, Bohème^{TM}
Turin, Italy

Puccini was nobody's fool. After the first performance of La Bohème on 1 February 1896 at the Teatro Regio, Turin, he and his manager, Giulio Ricordi (who was also his publisher), took a cue from Stendhal: combination marketing. This is exactly what they did.

It all started when Puccini was looking for a conductor for *La Bohème.* Although Puccini preferred a famous conductor, he accepted Ricordi's recommendation of a young rather eccentric conductor by the name of Arturo Toscanini. The premiere was a success, though not as successful as *Manon Lescaut.* Though the critics gave it luke warm reviews, it was a hit with the public and with each performance gained a bigger and bigger following concluding with a major production in Palermo.

Within a few years, the opera was selling out to pack audiences throughout Europe. Even Mahler, who had recently been hired as the conductor of the Vienna Court Opera, was dispatched to Venice in May 1897 to hear a performance of both Leoncavallo and Puccini. When he returned he declared Puccini to be the better of the two and after Mahler took over as director of the Court Opera, he produced Puccini's *Bohème* in 1903.

So how did Puccini take advantage of his opera's popularity? It can be traced to something Mimi says in the opera: "When ice and snow are thawing, when days begin to mellow, mine is the warming kiss of April, So tender! Mine are the first rays of sunshine! I watch as the rose starts to open. Slowly petal by petal. How sweet to breathe the perfume of a flower! The flowers I fondly sew, my embroidered flowers." But it wasn't flowers he was thinking about, but perfume. Recalling Stendhal's success, he worked out an agreement with Henri Murger's estate to get the publishing rights to the novel, *Bohemians of the Latin Quarter,* on which he based his opera. Then, he contacted some perfume people in the Napa Valley of California and closed a deal to have his opera become a perfume, a perfume that was characterized "as an artistic, passionate, and unabashed celebration of the senses." Its notes of Green Chypre were overtly feminine with a touch of the exotic. Its top notes were made from Bergamot, Lemon, Pepper, Rosewood, Neroli, and Galbanum; its Mid Notes of Rose Geranium, Orris, Lily, White Rose, Bulgarian Rose, Carnation, Grandiflorum Jasmine, Honey, Lilac, and Clove Bud and its Base Notes of Tolu and Peru Blossom, Siam and Virginia Cedars, Amber, Sandalwood, Frankincense, Patchouli, Myrrh, Tobacco and Tree Moss. The unique, French, oval-shaped, frosted bottle was gracefully tied with a bias-cut, hand-dyed ribbon. A rose-gold, stamped metal charm hangs from the ribbon. The entire packaging reflects a light open-armed approach to life.

But Puccini didn't stop there. He really wanted to outdo Stendhal and with that in mind contacted the Montblanc pen makers and worked a deal to create the "Montblanc Bohème Collection" a collection that "combines elements of modern design with the traditional values and craftsmanship for which Montblanc is known. It was created for a new generation of people who have a contemporary lifestyle and who appreciate non-traditional luxury products. This sleek and stylish collection, which feels luxurious in the hand, is more jewels that write than writing instruments and is destined to become the next icon of popular culture. Elegantly shaped with a flat top, small size, and crafted of sleek black resin, the Montblanc Bohème features a jewel in the clip – a touch of decadence and extravagant excess."

What happened after that was sheer marketing genius. At every performance, Puccini had the novel, the perfume and the pen elegantly wrapped together with papers designed by Tassotti. Needless to say, Puccini became a multi-millionaire and invested heavily in an American Baseball Club named the Smoked Italians: a team that later became known as the Pittsburgh Pirates.

Dalí's Laguna™

Dalí's Laguna™
Figueres, Spain

D alí was a perfervid enthusiast of his work and became all things to Dalí: compañera, muse, model. What an exquisite oxymoron: Dalí Perfume. It's even more Dalíesque than Dalí. It's common knowledge that by 1929 Dalí, along with people like Breton and Buñuel, was in the vanguard of the Surrealist movement. Three decades later his work was extraordinarily popular, but it was only after he married Gala Eluard in 1958 that he actually entertained the idea of expanding into the perfume business. When Dalí met Gala, she was married to the French poet, Paul Eluard. Ten years Dalí's senior, she important, she became his business manager and it was only after he painted *Gala Nude From Behind Looking in an Invisible Mirror, 1960,* that Gala came up with the idea.

It is now common knowledge that Dalí was impotent and that he had a horror of female genitalia, but in order to try to deal with the former problem, Gala devised a plan. Before she posed for the painting, Gala took a lingering bath in which she added a mixture of mandarin, peach and lemon plus rosewood, orris and lily of the valley. When she climbed out she then used some oil of vanilla mixed with amber and musk. To say the very least, Dalí had a difficult keeping his mind on the painting as he stood there looking at the elegant lines of Gala's back and smelling the sensual scent of that mélange of odors. In his diary, he records that the combination of chemicals plus the vision of Gala's ass actually gave him an erection. Spurred on by that result, the always resourceful Gala figured that if it worked for Dalí who was impotent, perhaps it would work for others. Taking a clue from Bach, Gala put all those chemicals together and decided to market the product as a perfume. The name "Laguna" was chosen for obvious reasons and the perfume hit the market in the mid-60s and has maintained incredible popularity since. But Gala also understood the "other side" of Dalí and she knew of his undying love for Lorca. As a tribute to that, she also came up with a fragrance for men in hopes that any male dysfunction would be taken care of the same way.

De Musset's Pôeme™

De Musset's Pôeme™
Paris, France

The question most everyone asks is what's the connection between Alfred de Musset and Lancôme? The answer, of course, lay in the mystery of Musset's poetry and perhaps we need to begin with his love affair with George Sand.

George was a very lonely woman. Approaching 30 and alone she asked here dear friend, Sainte-Beuve to fix her up. She had already had love failures with Sandea and Merimée so when Sainte-Beuve suggested the 22-year old Musset she refused saying he was too much of a dandy for her. He tried to fix her up with Dumas, but they didn't hit it off. Feeling horribly despondent, she finally met Musset at a dinner thrown by François Buloz, editor of the *Revue des Deux Mondes.* Through a series of letters, their relationship intensified culminating in the following letter he wrote to her: "Dear George, I have something terribly foolish to tell you. I should have said it on the return from our walk, but instead, like an ass, I merely write it. I am in love with you and I have been ever since the first time I went to your house. I know that you have already been in love, that you are kind, and I put my trust in you. Adieu George, I love you as if I were your child." Several days later, he wrote her a poem *To Love* that contains these verses:

> Jamais amant aime mourant sur sa maîtresse
> N'a dans deux yeux plus noirs bu la céleste ivresse,
> Nul ur un plus beau front ne t'a jamais baisé.

Her response was passionately forthcoming as Sand wrote to Sainte-Beuve, "I am in love, and this time most seriously, with Alfred de Musset." Soon thereafter, Musset moved in with her at 19 Quai Malaquais. There's no need to go into the details of their passionate liaison or the anguish of their separation. But words were not enough for Musset to remember her by. Of an evening in April 1857, while playing a game of piquet with his Uncle Desherbiers, Musset asked him if he were to leave something eternal for the woman he loved most deeply, what would it be? His uncle thought for a moment and said, "The scent of words." It was then that Musset had the idea of creating a scent that would last forever as a poem to his major love, George Sand.

Sadly, it didn't happen for him, but on the morning of 1 May 1857, while dying and bedridden, Musset called for his uncle. In a whisper, he reminded him of what he had said the month before. Desherbiers nodded. He then asked Desherbiers to do him the favor of creating a scent for George. "And what would you want me to call it?" Desherbiers asked. Musset merely smiled and said, "Poême" and then expired. It then became Desherbiers's charge to make manifest Musset's request. It was a long and arduous process, costly. But Desherbiers succeeded and the perfume was released on 8 June 1876, the same day George Sand died. After Desherbiers' death, the company went into financial troubles only to be reinvigorated by Desherbiers's nephew and in 1928 Poême was relaunched in a Maurice Depinoix designed bottle with the following poem inscribed in the glass:

A George Sand (VI)

Porte ta vie ailleurs, ô toi qui fus ma vie ;
Verse ailleurs ce trésor que j'avais pour tout bien.
Va chercher d'autres lieux, toi qui fus ma patrie,
Va fleurir, ô soleil, ô ma belle chérie,
Fais riche un autre amour et souviens-toi du mien.
Laisse mon souvenir te suivre loin de France ;
Qu'il parte sur ton coeur, pauvre bouquet fané,
Lorsque tu l'as cueilli, j'ai connu l'Espérance,
Je croyais au bonheur, et toute ma souffrance
Est de l'avoir perdu sans te l'avoir donné.

Today, the bottle does not exist, nor do the words, but the scent of the words still exists remaining a testimony to Musset's enduring love for George Sand.

Nerval's Bain Mouissant™
Paris, France

One look at Nerval's face and you might imagine that he never liked to bathe. And you'd be right. Not by choice, but by circumstance since Nerval was constantly on the move with never a place to call his own. But, at the same time, Nerval was an absolute fanatic about cleanliness. A glance at the titles of some of his poems should give you a clue: *Être sans condemnation; Être blanc; Être pauvre; Être à Blanc; Être sans arme* just to name a few gives you a clean idea about his personality. And then there are these lines from *Sylvie*, "I left the theatre where I sat every evening in a stage box, dressed with the elegance and care befitting my hopes." Could these be the lines of a scrofulant? In Gautier's ironically titled, *À lui la sale besogne (I Leave All The Dirty Work to Him)*, Gautier not only discusses how he and Nerval came up with the idea for basketball (See: *Borges' Travel, Hemingway's Garage*), but discusses how the two of them came up with the idea for Bain Moussaint. Of course, it all related to a woman: Jenny Colon.

It's common knowledge that Nerval was absolutely smitten with the actor, Jenny Colon and he had admired her from afar. According to Gautier, she was a pretty blond with broad forehead, delicate, aquiline nose, sparkling brown eyes under pale, velvety eyebrows, well-chiseled, smiling mouth with a mocking curve on the lower lip which lent it peculiar charm, a small dimple in the center of her chin that seemed like loves' nest, and a white, delicate complexion, silky and pulpy, like a camellia leaf or rice paper. It, too, was Gautier who fixed introduced them, but before that happened, Nerval was absolutely distraught at the possibility of his appearance and "smelling bad." But what were his options?

The always resourceful Gautier remembered that Baudelaire often used a bubble bath when he first met Marie Daubrun. He contacted Baudelaire who, by that time, was staying at the hotel of the same name, and the former told him it was an Oak Moss Bubble Bath that, according to Baudelaire, "was a real turn on." Of course, Gautier was rather skeptical of that since Charles was not as big an "ass man" as he thought, but he immediately rushed out and bought a bottle of the bubble bath figuring anything was better than having Nerval smell as if he were dumped in the St. Martin Canal.

At first, Nerval was reluctant. A bubble bath? For Nerval? "But how many times do you first meet Jenny Colon?" Gautier asked. It was a clinching argument and Nerval rushed off to the tub. The hour came and Nerval was about as anxious as any man could be, but it was a bittersweet moment. She told him that she could not love another since she was in love with someone else. But Nerval, like Turgenev and Pauline Viardot, was wont to give her up and he assumed the role of a Platonic paramour for almost two years writing her beautiful letters telling her that "You are the first woman I love and I am, perhaps, the first man to love you to such a degree. If this is not a sort of marriage blessed by the heavens, then the word love is an empty word. Let it be a true marriage then, in which the bride yields saying: This is the hour!" Unfortunately, it wasn't to be. Everyone knew it including the always perspicacious

Gautier since on 11 April 1838, Jenny Colon married Louis-Marie-Gabriel Leplus and settled down in Paris. As Nerval was to have said later, "it was the most anguishing, the most terrible blow that destiny can strike the soul . . . one must then resolve to live or to die." Four years later, 5 June 1842, Jenny Colon, aged 34, died and on 1 November 1842, Nerval walked with other mourners to the cemetery at Montmarte. He wrote down the location of her tomb, no. 1, 22nd division, and locked it away with her last letter and a lock of her hair. And every day from that moment on, until he died on the bitterly cold night on the rue de la Vielle Lanterne, Nerval would stand in front of the cemetery at Montmarte and try to sell bottles of Oak Moss Bubble Bath pitching it with the words, "There can be no greater cleansing than the cleansing of a heart with the bath of Sheba." Truer words were never spoken.

Sisley's Eau de Soir™

Sisley's Eau Du Soir™
Paris, France

What can we make of Sisley? The French impressionist landscape painter, born in Paris of English parents who was a founding member of the Impressionists, but seemed to lack all the excitement in his life that his contemporaries had. At first, Sisley attempted a career in business, but failed. In 1862, he went to study with Gleyre where he met other painters such as Renoir, Monet and Bazille. At Chailly, he painted with Monet, at Marlotte with Renoir. At the time, his painting was deeply influenced by Courbet, and when he first exhibited at the Salon in 1867 it was as the pupil of Corot.

Things were looking up for Sisley until he got the telegram from his father indicating that he had lost all his money as a result of the Franco-Prussian war. Suddenly, Sisley was impoverished. No brother Theo to bail him out, Sisley was horribly distraught. Then, quite by accident, he read about what Monet was doing in order to raise capital (See: *Borges' Travel, Hemingway's Garage*). Flushed with the thought that Monet might be of some help to him and his family, he met Monet in Paris where the latter gave him the idea of investing in perfumes. At first, Sisley was perplexed. "Perfumes? What does that have to do with painting?" Monet responded,

"Yeah, and what do pearls have to do with painting?" It was an irrefutable argument. Through Monet's connections they found a perfume manufacturer in Paris and Sisley spent hours upon hours trying to find the right scent. Once he found the right scent, he spent hours and hours trying to come up with a name. And that's when destiny arrived.

Sisley happened to be working on his painting, *The Saint-Martin Canal in Paris. 1870.* He was walking home one evening, after spending the better part of the day smelling scents, when he sat down by the canal. Sisley never painted night scenes. All his landscapes were painted predominately in the afternoon, preferably with sun. He was looking into the canal, tossing stones into it, when the thought suddenly came to him: eau du soir. So excited, he rushed home to tell his wife who was boiling potatoes for the tenth night in a row. The following day he told Monet of the idea and he was as enthusiastic as Sisley was. With both a scent and a name all that remained was a release date and on 31 March 1872 he unveiled *Eau du Soir* at an exhibit in Montmartre. Not only was the exhibit a success, but the perfume was a sensation and soon people were asking Sisley if he had any ideas about fashion as well. In fact, he did and with the money he made from both he retired to Moret-sur-Loing where for the rest of his life he painted landscapes.

Stendhal's White Wear™

Stendhal's White Wear™
Paris, France

What else would one expect from someone who wrote *De L'Amour?* It was only a matter of time before Stendhal would hit on the idea of packaging the book with some skincare and anti-aging creams as a way to increase the mass sales of both. Genius. Pure marketing genius.

Let's begin with where this journey actually begins . . . Stendhal's women. Henri didn't have a lot of luck with the ladies. Oh, he had his share, but nothing really to write home about. As others have commented, Henri was no Casanova, certainly no Sade and not even a bon Vivant-Denon. Presumably, the book was written to exorcise himself from the *Weltschmerz* he suffered at the arms and hands of one Metilde Dembowski. Their relationship, such as it was, ended after he was booted from Milan by Metternicht's police in 1821 when he was already 38. Sometime after that, he contracted syphilis and, well, that kind of put a damper on his sex life. Not to be diffused, Stendhal returned to Paris in an attempt to gain some literary notoriety in the salons. During this period he had an affair with Countess Clémentine Curial, who wrote over 200 letters to Beyle in two years. In 1822 Stendhal published *De L'Amour* which some contend was based on the psychology of Destutt de Tracy the liberal French nobleman Destutt de Tracy who sought to extend Enlightenment liberalism to post-Revolutionary France. Destutt de Tracy's main work was the series *Eléments d'idéologie* (1801-1815) which followed up on the philosophy, psychology and economics of Condillac. Like Condillac, Destutt de Tracy sought to ground value in psychology, particularly utility. Stendhal regarded himself as a disciple of de Tracy, and perhaps borrowed from him the classificatory, cataloguing spirit with which he started the book. But I'm getting away from the facts.

On Love was not a best-seller and he needed to find a way to make it one. As a matter of fact, Stendhal once wrote in the preface, "THIS book has met with no success; it has been found unintelligible, and not without cause. In this new edition, therefore, the author has tried above all to express his ideas clearly. He has related how they occurred to him, and has written a preface and an introduction, all for the sake of clarity. Yet despite all this care, for every hundred readers who have enjoyed *Corinne*, not more than four will understand this book.

Although it deals with love, this little book is not a novel, and above all, it's not as entertaining as a novel. It is simply an exact and scientific description of a brand of madness very rare in France. The conventions, whose sway holds daily, more from a fear of ridicule than from moral purity, have turned the word which serves me for a title into something unmentionable, something that even conveys lewdness. I could not avoid using the word, and trust that the scientific austerity of my style puts me beyond reproach on that score. . ."

Distraught, Stendhal wrote the Countess and that's where the Countess came in. It was Curial's idea that Stendhal package the book differently. Stendhal who was about as interested in the marketing component of book selling as he was in keeping his own name[15] basically gave the entire project to Curial and it was she who came up with the first sample of Stendhal care products which included the now well-known, Aqua Purete, the Hydro-Harmony Moisturizing Cream Mask, and the ever-popular, Whitewear Whitening Serum. The combination was an extraordinary success and became a packaging blockbuster that Balzac envied so much he tried to emulate it, but as with most of Balzac's business projects, it failed. But that was just the beginning for Stendhal. Once the book and the facial products took off he and Curial moved on to the hotel business where things only got better. (See: *Le Stendhal Hôtel, Paris*).

---

15 Mr. Myself, Leiméry, Mr. de Léry, Auguste, Alceste, Tempète, L Roux, Chapuis, Collar. Favier, Dupuy, Fauris Saint-Bard, Dubois of Bée, D. Gruffo Papers, C Simonetta, c.f. ainé Ravet, Harry, George Simple, Z Joseph Charrin, Hor. Of Cluny, Expensive. De Cutendre, Chomont, Servant boys, Periner, Count Change, Baron Relguir, Count de Chablis, Dupellée, Chauvin, Lunenbourg, Louis-Alexandre César Bombet, Hector C C Bombet, Domenica Junius, Banti, Choppin D' Ornouville, Condotti 48, Capeva, Cotonet, Costes, Casimir, Caumartin, Blaise Durand, Durand-Robet, Timoléon Tisset, Timoléon Gaillard, Timoléon Brenet, Timoléon Of Wood, Sphinx, Baron Raisinet, Baron Dormant, Baron Boudon, Baron Patault, Seymours, Don Phlegm, Poruth, Anastase of Serpière, Leonce D., Adolphe de Seyssels, Jules Pardessus, Al Feburier, Is. Ich. Charlier, Gaillard, Meynier, Roger, Tamboust, Mequillet, Chomont, General Pellet, Machiavelli B, Old Hummums, William Crocodile, Horace Smith, Edmond de Charency, Porcheron, A. L. Capello, Border It, Chappier of Ilets, Chincilla, P. F Piouf, Polype Coils-Puff, Of ainé Palice-intrailles, Lavardin, Duversy, Ths. Jefferson, Rowe, Besanc., CH de Saupiquet, Tombouctou, Poverino, Smith & Co.

Vigny's Beau Catcher™

Vigny's Beau Catcher™
Paris, France

How can one think of perfume and not think of Vigny? One of the most foremost romantics of his age, he was a military man for much of his life until that fateful night of 30 May 1829 when, after attending a performance of Delavigne's *Marino Faliero*, Vigny was introduced to the actress, Marie Dorval. After that meeting, all bets were off. She was 31; he was 32, but their sexual experiences were not equal. She debuted in Paris in 1818 and by 1822 she was a Parisian favorite. Vigny was merely a child in comparison to her and Sainte-Beuve once declared that whenever Vigny was in her presence he was under a "perpetual seraphic hallucination." She too felt overwhelmed by her own love for Vigny and became his muse. Oddly enough for the next two years, Vigny wrote very little, so consumed was he by her presence. This was only a few years before George Sand would fall in love with Musset so it was with more than a dash of irony that she said about Dorval and Vigny, "Oh, naïve et passionate, et jeune et suave, et tremblante et terrible." However towards the end of 1835 Vigny discovered what the rest of Paris had already known; namely, Dorval had been lasciviously unfaithful to him. And with whom? No one other than Alexandre Dumas!

What resulted was something extraordinary. Not only did Vigny retreat into a life of reclusivity, into a life divorced from family and friends, but he never forgave Dorval. During the last years of his life, he retreated to his country house called Le Maine-Giraud and there became obsessed with practicing the art of perfume making. But as we discover in his journal[16] Vigny was not experimenting to discover the most fragrant scent, but something else, something that would parallel the vitriol he held for Dorval.

He practiced incessantly trying to come up with the right mix of essential oils in an attempt to make smell that would parallel his feelings. He experimented with a number of base notes (the most long-lasting scent), the middle notes (the second longest), and top notes (that which evaporates first). But because oils all evaporate at different rates, he could never get the exact mixture until he had a dream and in the dream the mixture came to him: cassia, with its spicy, pungent red hot aroma; myrrh, with its hot, bitter pungency; and the oddest of ingredients, basil. Awakened in the middle of the night, Vigny rushed to his laboratory where he made the concoction, a scent that was at the same time disturbing and intoxicating.

So obsessed was Vigny, that he tracked down the father of the great French glass maker, Emile Galle, Charles Galle who owned a glass factory in Nancy. He commissioned Galle to come up with a one-of-a-kind bottle that would hold the "perfume" Vigny invented. Galle was only too willing to assist the poet. But by then, Vigny was diagnosed with cancer so he was frantic to get the mixture made and delivered to Dorval. Galle did what he could and on 15 September 1863, he delivered the bottle with the title, "Beau

---

16 *The Death of Dorval: Vigny.* Translated from the French by Mark Axelrod. Tallahassee: Fiction Collective 2, 2003.

Catcher" to a bedridden Vigny. Two days later, Vigny died, but lived long enough to know that Madame Dorval received what he once called, "the languishing perfume of a love lost and labored."

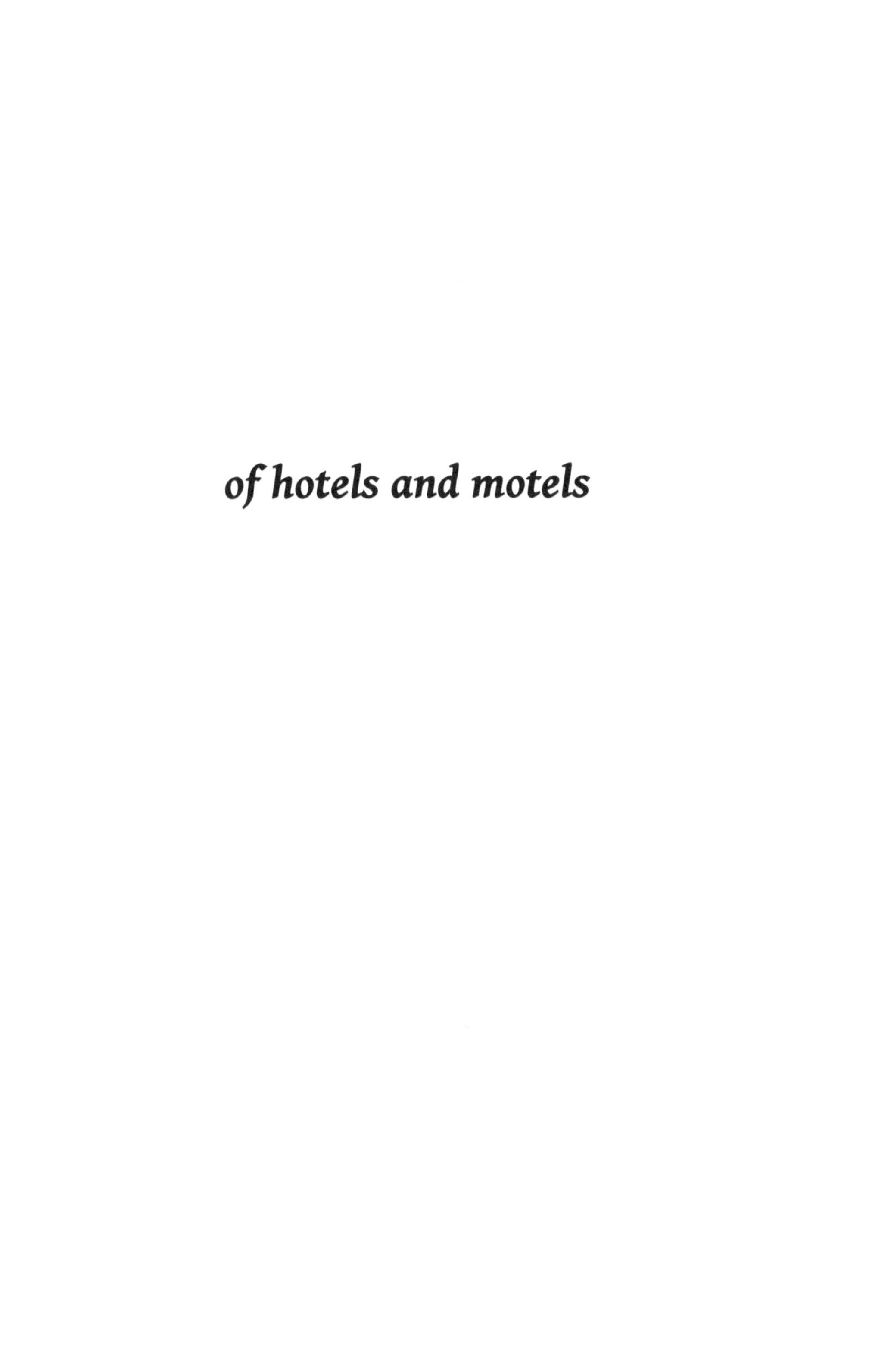

of hotels and motels

Baudelaire Bastille Hôtel

Baudelaire Hôtel Bastille™
Paris, France

I mean, what other hardships was poor Charles to endure! The whole thing began in Paris while writing his Spleen poems. One wet and foggy afternoon, after gazing out his window at a nearby graveyard, Charles turned to see his mangy, half-starved cat attempting to sleep upon the frigid tiles of his garret as a smoke-shrouded, wet log hissed horribly in the fireplace. "What," he thought to himself, "am I doing in this place?" Fed up with the cold and the frigid hunger, he took to looking at the stack of legal papers his stepfather, General Aupick, had drawn up with his lawyer, Ancelle, to create this life of penury for him. "God save me, there must be a loophole somewhere!" he declared in one of his journals.[17] It's common knowledge that on his majority in 1842 he moved into a flat in the Hôtel Lauzun on the Ile St-Louis and tended to fritter away a lot of money. In an attempt to reduce his debt, his step-father hired Ancelle as his financial guardian. Unfortunately, they didn't eliminate all of his debt and put him on a paltry monthly income which is the state in which we found him.

In a letter to Ancelle, written in February, 1866, Baudelaire said:

---

17 *Quel Emmerdement! Notes on Accelle.* Charles Baudelaire. Translated from the French by Mark Axelrod.

"Faut-il vous dire, à vous qui ne l'avez pas plus deviné que les autres, que dans ce livre atroce j'ai mis tout mon coeur, toute ma tendresse, toute ma religion (travestie), toute ma haine? Il est vrai que j'écrirai le contraire, que je jurerai mes grands dieux que c'est un livre d'art pur, de signerie, de jonglerie, et je mentirai comme un arracheur de dents." He then spent the better part of two days, scouring the stack of legal documents, suffering, without sleep, without food, without wine, without hash, until he found what he thought would finally evict him from his horrible state of impecunity. At last, his limited legal studies availed him.

At about 3 a.m. on the 2nd day, Baudelaire discovered the following line in the trust form established by his step-father and Ancelle.

§4. 075 Successor Trustees: In the event of the death or incapacity of any trustee, I hereby nominate and appoint as successor trustee Theophile Gautier. In the event the successor trustee does not serve I appoint whomever shall at the time be the first designated beneficiary hereunder. Incapacity is hereby defined as the inability to conduct business transactions for a period of, but not limited to, two working days. The successor trustee will, at that time, assume any and all trustee decisions and may allocate any funds and/or property as he deems necessary.

Baudelaire was overjoyed by the discovery since it meant that if either his stepfather or his financial guardian got sick he could call upon Gautier to get him out of his financial bind! Needless to say, he tried everything in his power to get one of them sick going as far as recommending that his stepfather take his mother on a trip to Orient at which time he knew there was an influenza outbreak.

Nothing seemed to work for him until a cold and bleak March 31st when General Aupick came down with tonsillitis. Baudelaire seized the moment and rushed to Ancelle's office. As Gautier writes: "Baudelaire burst into Ancelle's room waving the trust form as if he were waving the French flag and screaming that the trust had to be honored and that Section 4.075 declared that if either Ancelle or Aupick were sick that I would then assume the task of successor trustee. Ancelle was beside himself. He looked over the document and there in black and white was exactly what Baudelaire claimed. Ancelle had no choice. He contacted me and asked me to meet with he and Baudelaire at a time convenient for all of us. Charles said immediately and so I had to drop everything I was doing, meant I had to delay the closing of a loan for my furniture business, to meet with them. But before I met with them, I met with Charles at the room where he was staying in the Hôtel Chiotte. He told me that if he didn't get out of those lodgings he'd die and since I was the successor trustee it was up to me to do so. "What can I do?" I asked. And he told me that Aupick had a major investment in a hotel in Paris. "What hotel?" I asked. "The Baudelaire Bastille Hotel located at 12, Rue De Charonne." "But," I said, "I've never heard of it?" He told me Aupick renamed it for his mother, Caroline, and the name had only recently changed. I asked him what it was called before and he said "the Hotel California." "The same as the Eagles?" I asked. "The same," he answered. I asked him what he wanted me to recommend to Ancelle and he said that he be allowed to live there permanently. I agreed and because of section 4.075 in the trust agreement Ancelle had to concur."

Baudelaire was thrilled. He felt that his life was going to change for the better. Unfortunately, the loophole only allowed him to live decently, but not to eliminate his debt and so for the rest of his life he was able to live in the hotel after his name, but never to escape his debt. Perhaps that was what the Eagles meant when they said, "Relax said the night man, we are programmed to receive, you can check out any time you like, but you can never leave." Perhaps too that's what prompted him to write, "In every climate and under every sun, Death laughs at you, mad mortals, as you run; And often perfumes herself with myrrh, like you And mingles with your madness, irony!" Ironically, it was the syphilis he acquired from his affair with Jeanne Duval in the same hotel that was to release him from his future cares and it was Gautier who had to commit him to a Paris nursing home for the last year of his life. The hotel still remains on 12 Rue De Charonne and above the room that Baudelaire slept in is a sign that reads: Welcome, hypocrite reader —my fellow—my brother!

Hôtel Claude Bernard

Hôtel Claude Bernard
Paris, France

So when is a hotel not a hotel? When it's a laboratory. As is common knowledge, Bernard started off a man of letters, but ended up a man of medicine. His *Introduction a la medecine experimentale* (*Introduction to Experimental Medicine*) (1865) stands as one of the major achievements of modern medicine. His thesis: how fact and idea collaborate in experimental research. But not everyone approved. As a matter of fact, a lot of people disapproved of his methods. But the history of the hotel is absolutely fascinating.

He wrote:

> . . . we must of necessity go down to objective reality . . . In the search for truth by the experimental method, feeling always takes the lead: it begets the a priori idea or intuition: reasoning develops the idea and deduces its logical consequences. But if feeling must be clarified by reason, reason must in turn be guided by experiment.

Unsurprisingly, Bernard was a firm exponent of vivisection and was a skillful practitioner when necessary. It is not true that his holistic view of creatures revealed duplicity in his outlook on vivisection, even though he did write that it was impossible to understand the functioning of dissected organs and tissues. His point was that they could only be completely understood in the whole functioning animal as they contributed to the "precise and informed" relationships that maintained the regulated constancy of the *milieu interieur*.

His academic advances were so spectacular that in 1854, a personal chair was created for him at the Sorbonne and in the following year he succeeded to the chair of experimental physiology at the College. It was at that time, the history of the hotel took on major significance.

The Sorbonne had no laboratory, but eventually Bernard met the Emperor Napoleon III who was so impressed by him and his work he promised to build him a laboratory at the Sorbonne, but, in the meantime, he offered to build one in an abandoned hotel located at 43 rue des Écoles, only blocks from the Sorbonne itself. And it was in that hotel, on the top floor, that he wrote and revised his "Leçons", seventeen volumes of lectures devoted to various topics in physiology, and where he conducted the vast number of experiments that not only paved his way to becoming a member of the Senate, but to his admission into the Académie des Sciences.

Victor Hugo Inn

Victor Hugo Inn
Laguna Beach, California

A h, the continuing saga of Victor Hugo. As you may recall *(See: Borges' Travel, Hemingway's Garage)*, Hugo was having all sorts of legal problems with the Disney Corporation. In court, out of court, settlements, non-settlements, things became so litigious that Disney once thought of naming one of its rides, *Adjudication Mountain.*[18] Seems like Hugo was involved in everything, but writing. But like all novels as well as Disney™ films, there had to be an end to it.

Hugo's is a continuing saga and one none of us would have expected otherwise knowing the genius. But to talk about the inn one really needs to talk about how it all started. Though much of this can be read in *Borges' Travel, Hemingway's Garage*, it would be wise to recap the events preceding the purchase of the inn.

Hugo was never very poor. Nor was he short of recognition. So this article is more of an *homage* to what actually happened to Notre-Dame and the hunchback who used to live there. At the age of fifteen, Hugo had already been acknowledged by the French Academy for his poetry and by seventeen he had won awards from the Jeux floraux de Toulouse. And, perhaps, because of that success

---

18 This ride eventually became known as "Thunder Mountain."

the problem for Hugo was not so much to make money, but how to invest it. And that need to diversify established one of the most fascinating of events in literary history. As most everyone is well aware, the mature Hugo was extremely interested in the metaphysical and at the age of fifty he became intrigued by séances. Coincidentally, it was at the same time he went into exile from France due, in large measure, to his vilification of Louis Napoléon. In 1853, exiled with his family (i.e. wife, children, mistress), Hugo retreated to the British Isles first to Jersey then to Guernsey. It was in Guernsey that the table-rapping séances began.

At first, the séances proved fruitless. That is, nothing happened except for a lot of table rapping which merely resulted in headaches for *the maestro*. As a matter of fact, he was reputed to have said after the first séance, "Ça ne vaut pas un pet de lapin" or "how disappointing." But after continued séances, a spirit did speak to him. In fact, it was his dead daughter, Léopoldine, and her message was truly prophetic. These séances were all documented and one of the most mysterious of messages Hugo received from his daughter was the following: "Quasimodo will leave Notre-Dame for Anaheim."[19] The statement initially made no sense to Hugo who had visited Anaheim (located in the Ruhr Valley of Germany), but only on his way to Warsaw as part of a book tour. He virtually dismissed the statement until 1876 when, after being elected to the Senate, he met, in Paris, at the Café Dauphin, an American by the name of Rudolph Eisner who said he represented a fledgling cartoon company[20] in the United States. Now film was merely in its fetal stages in France as Lumière and Méliès were not to have

---

19 *The Séances of Victor Hugo*. Paris: Flammarion, 1985.
20 The company, of course, was originally called "The Willie Company" and went on to become the present day Disney™ Studios.

produced anything for another decade, but Eisner was interested in making an animated cartoon out of Hugo's *Notre-Dame de Paris* (1831). Hugo was rather fascinated by the idea and asked Eisner where this company was located.

"Burbank," he said, "but that's where our studio is. We plan to build a theme park in California."

"Where?" Hugo asked.

"Anaheim," was the answer.

And Hugo suddenly remembered the prophetic words of his dead daughter, "Quasimodo will leave Notre Dame for Anaheim and will then reside in the hills of Beverly." Flushed with the idea that his novel would be adapted to an animated cartoon, Eisner and Hugo worked out the contractual arrangements and a date was set for production.[21] But Hugo was still mystified by the future residence of Quasimodo in the hills of Beverly. What could that mean?

Almost six years later, 1882, Hugo sent his mistress, Juliette Drouet, to the United States to do some advanced booking for his latest novel *Torquemada*. When Eisner discovered she was in New York, he arranged for her to come to California to see the Willie Studios and to view what progress had been made on what had now been re-titled *Willie's Hunchback of Notre Dame*. She agreed. In a letter dated 2 December 1882, postmarked Burbank, Juliette writes Hugo: *"Good morning, my divine, adored love. This separation spares me no sorrow. Being away from you is like being rendered soulless, joyless, loveless, but I do these things for you not out of gratitude, but out my strongest, deepest love for you. Monsieur Eisner has shown me the animated drawings of Quasimodo. Somehow I do not think them what you*

---

21 Little did either Eisner or Hugo know that because of financial and technical problems the film wouldn't appear for another 120 years.

had in mind, but he tells me that is what the American public wants. Que dommage. He has also mentioned something to me about a restaurant in Beverly Hills, but I shall find out more later. My darling, this separation cannot be over too soon and I pray your love will take me from here to there with speed and sanctity. I love you, Juliette."

The restaurant Drouet alluded to was actually going out of business and Eisner convinced Hugo, through Drouet, to invest in it with the sound reasoning that it would diversify Hugo's portfolio. So convinced, he did in fact invest and the restaurant opened as the Victor Hugo Restaurant in 1883 the exact day Juliette Drouet died. If that were not irony enough, the restaurant burned to the ground in 1885 on the exact day Hugo was buried in the Panthéon. Some say it was the spirit of Quasimodo that burned the restaurant as an homage to the *maestro* since witnesses swear that on the night of fire they saw a hunchback rushing from the burning building. Others attest it was done by a disgruntled Willie employee who was fired after an altercation with the head of the animation studio who proclaimed that he had pornographized all that Willie had done.[22] In either case, all that remained was a matchbook cover which has since found its way into the Smithsonian.

But the spirit of Quasimodo lived on and not to everyone's liking. Certainly not the Hugo family and a relatively recent letter, signed by Charles, Adèle, Jeanne, Sophie and Léopoldine Hugo, denounced the "commercial debauchery which confuses the universality of genius with vulgar globalization by unscrupulous

---

22 This may have been the case as any casual scrutinizing of the video jacket of "The Little Mermaid" would attest. Andersen's outrage at the video jacket even caught the attention of his nemesis, Kierkegaard, who actually came to Andersen's defense in a monograph titled, *Dømmer Selv! Til Selvprøvelse Samtiden anbefalet* or *Judge For Yourselves! Recommended to the present time for Self-Examination.*

merchants." As Adèle Hugo-Chabrol said, "We are not after money. We are in favor of screen adaptations because they help new readers discover the author. But this time, Victor Hugo is not even mentioned on the posters." Alas it was true. Nowhere on any of the film posters of the Hunchback of Notre-Dame was Hugo's name mentioned which was in direct violation of the codicil that Hugo had signed with Rudolph Eisner.[23] Need less to say, the current Disney™ legal conundrum was in direct violation of that testimony.

This brings us to where we are now. As we know from the novel, *The Posthumous Memoirs of Blase Kubash,* Quasimodo is homeless and living in Paris; Esmeralda was forced to take on a job in soft porn movies in Hollywood. And Hugo? Well, apparently the Disney™ people decided to settle out of court. Though the figures were never disclosed, both *Variety* and the *Hollywood Reporter* reported that Hugo settled for something in the millions, certainly enough for him to open the Victor Hugo Inn in Laguna and to settle there to avoid the long and lugubrious Paris winters. If one looks closely, one can see him in the gardens of a December day, gazing out onto the Laguna Beaches as if recalling his days in Guernsey.

---

23 The codicil indicated that on any merchandising of *The Hunchback of Notre-Dame,* Hugo rightfully would be given top billing. The codicil was read and approved by Mr. Eisner.

Hôtel Lamartine

Hôtel Lamartine
Paris, France

If there's a hotel involved, you can bet there's a woman involved as well. Not any different with Lamartine. If Musset had his George Sand and Stendhal had his Countess Clémentine Curial and Baudelaire had his Jeanne Duval, then Lamartine would have his Elvire. But Elvire is a mystery. But just who was this Elvire and what was her influence? The answer has come in a tantalizing book titled, *Lamartine and the Lady of the Lake.*[24]

According to Culbute, in September 1816, Lamartine went to Aix-les-Bains to take the baths for a liver ailment. Actually, it wasn't a liver ailment merely hypochondria, an illness that was chronic for Lamartine. Now Lamartine happened to be staying at a boarding house in Aix in which a certain Julie Charles, née Bouchard des Hérettes (aka Mme Charles) also happened to be residing. Madame Charles was married to a very influential, albeit much older, man who was considered one of France's greatest savants. M. Charles was almost 40 years her senior. Regardless, what transpired was what anyone would have expected . . . they fell in love. She became his muse. A brief stroll with Julie on the shores of Lake Bourget and we get this:

---

24 *Lamartine and the Lady of the Lake.* Hélène Culbute. Paris: Flammarion, 2002.

Ainsi, toujours poussés vers de nouveaux rivages,
Dans la nuit éternelle emportés sans retour,
Ne pourrons-nous jamais sur l'océan des âges
Jeter l'ancre un seul jour?

Ô lac! l'année à peine a fini sa carrière,
Et près des flots chéris qu'elle devait revoir,
Regarde! je viens seul m'asseoir sur cette pierre
Où tu la vis s'asseoir!

Tu mugissais ainsi sous ces roches profondes;
Ainsi tu te brisais sur leurs flancs déchirés;
Ainsi le vent jetait l'écume de tes ondes
Sur ses pieds adorés.

Un soir, t'en souvient-il? nous voguions en silence;
On n'entendait au loin, sur l'onde et sous les cieux,
Que le bruit des rameurs qui frappaient en cadence
Tes flots harmonieux.

Tout à coup des accents inconnus à la terre
Du rivage charmé frappèrent les échos,
Le flot fut attentif, et la voix qui m'est chère
Laissa tomber ces mots:

«Ô temps, suspends ton vol! et vous, heures propices,
Suspendez votre cours!
Laissez-nous savourer les rapides délices
Des plus beaux de nos jours!

«Assez de malheureux ici-bas vous implorent;

Coulez, coulez pour eux;
Prenez avec leurs jours les soins qui les dévorent;
Oubliez les heureux.

«Mais je demande en vain quelques moments encore,
Le temps m'échappe et fuit;
Je dis à cette nuit: «Sois plus lente»; et l'aurore
Va dissiper la nuit.

«Aimons donc, aimons donc! de l'heure fugitive,
Hâtons-nous, jouissons!
L'homme n'a point de port, le temps n'a point de rive;
Il coule, et nous passons!»

Temps jaloux, se peut-il que ces moments d'ivresse,
Où l'amour à longs flots nous verse le bonheur,
S'envolent loin de nous de la même vitesse
Que les jours de malheur?

Hé quoi! n'en pourrons-nous fixer au moins la trace?
Quoi! passés pour jamais? quoi! tout entiers perdus?
Ce temps qui les donna, ce temps qui les efface,
Ne nous les rendra plus?

Éternité, néant, passé, sombres abîmes,
Que faites-vous des jours que vous engloutissez?
Parlez: nous rendrez vous ces extases sublimes
Que vous nous ravissez?

Ô lac! rochers muets! grottes! forêt obscure!
Vous que le temps épargne ou qu'il peut rajeunir,

> *Gardez de cette nuit, gardez, belle nature,*
> *Au moins le souvenir!*
>
> *Qu'il soit dans ton repos, qu'il soit dans tes orages,*
> *Beau lac, et dans l'aspect de tes riants coteaux,*
> *Et dans ces noirs sapins, et dans ces rocs sauvages*
> *Qui pendent sur tes eaux!*
>
> *Qu'il soit dans le zéphyr qui frémit et qui passe,*
> *Dans les bruits de tes bords par tes bords répétés,*
> *Dans l'astre au front d'argent qui blanchit ta surface*
> *De ses molles clartés!*
>
> *Que le vent qui gémit, le roseau qui soupire,*
> *Que les parfums légers de ton air embaumé,*
> *Que tout ce qu'on entend, l'on voit et l'on respire,*
> *Tout dise: «Ils ont aimé!»*

Not bad for an hour's work. But let's not dally. She was a few years Lamartine's senior and according to many, she was very sensual. Half Breton, half Creole, she seemed to exude a sensuality that was stifled due, in large part, to her husband's impotence. He, of course, thought she had a neurasthenic problem not a sexual one and sent her to the baths for a cure, but what she was cured of has seemed to be a mystery. But Culbute contends that's not the case and that Lamartine and Elvire had a passionate love affair. This speculation is borne out when Lamartine's speaks in his correspondence of "un culte idéal et passionate." They spent three weeks together and clearly they didn't spend all that time traipsing around a lake. When she left, Lamartine would pine away at his lost love, but they had made plans, assignations.

Julie and her husband inhabited an apartment in the French Institute in Paris where they conducted soirées with French celebrities. It just so happens that at one of those soirées, Lamartine was invited. When Lamartine entered, he stopped short. As Madame Duclaux recounts: "There she was standing by the mantelpiece, in the full light, her elbow indolently leaning on the slab of white marble, her slim figure, white shoulders and delicate profile doubled by the reflection in the mirror. She was leaning forward her head a little on one side, with parted lips, anxiously listening. She wore a gown of dull black silk, as black as her hair, hung over with black lace, round the line of her exposed breasts, the waist, the hem." So, try giving a poetry reading looking at her. It was difficult for Lamartine. So difficult that they eventually fled to the Hôtel Opera and there made love.

But their love was not to be. Only a year later, Julie died in Paris. Aymon de Virieu who was always their go-between brought the news to Lamartine as well as the crucifix which she kissed upon her death. Aymon also brought the news that it was her last wish that her husband buy the hotel in which she and Lamartine made love and to rename it in his name. The wish granted, the hotel remains today and their room, located on the floor above the lobby, allegedly still whispers:

> *"O lac! L'année à peine a finis a carrière,*
> *Et près des flots chéris qu'elle devait revoir,*
> *Regarde! Je viens seul m'asseoir sur cette Pierre*
> *Où tu la vis s'asseoir."*

Leonardo's Suites

Leonardo's Suites & DaVinci's Ristorante
Tustin, California

The origin of the motel is, well, astonishing. With the success of the restaurant, both Saltarelli and DaVinci decided to purchase some adjacent property and build a motel, but the origin of such a project is one of the most fascinating in DaVinci's brilliant career. It is common knowledge that Section XXXVIII of DaVinci's notebooks deals with architecture. What's fascinating is the recent discovery of the missing motel plans. Known only as "The Codex Albergo," it was considered lost until its miraculous discovery in Venice. The subsection [Architectural Drawings: ground plans] originally contained four sub-subsections: Buttery, Kitchen. Family. Motel. This is a copy of the original sketch of the Albergo which was the prototype for Leonardo's Suites.

Due to zoning problems with the City of Tustin, the plans had to be extensively revised to be in compliance with certain ordinances and the present motel has been reduced in size and scope to accommodate those ordinances. But the journey of the missing Albergo Codex is fascinating. It is common knowledge that the original manuscripts were passed on to Francesco Melzi to whom Leonardo bequeathed the manuscripts in his will dated 23 April 1518 "in return for the services and favours done him in the past." At Melzi's death, a certain Lelio Gavardi di Asola, a former tutor in the Melzi family, absconded with over a dozen manuscripts for the purpose of selling them to the Grand Duke Francesco of Florence. Unfortunately, the Duke died before the transaction could be accomplished and Gavardi went to Pisa trying to find a buyer.

Giovanni Mazzenta, a student of law at the University of Pisa, ran into Gavardi and the former tried to use him as a "fence" for the manuscripts. Outraged, Mazzenta told Gavardi that if he didn't return them to the Melzi family he would have him arrested. Garvardi agreed. To make a very long story, short, the Albergo Codex was discovered in 2001 in a copper container in the Venice basement of one Carlo Goldoni who subsequently put the manuscript up for auction when it was finally purchased by one William Gates III. Needless to say, the differences between the original motel as sketched in the Albergo Codex and the existing one are demonstrable, but any trip to Tustin would be incomplete without seeing DaVinci's Ristorante which is located on the corner of Tustin Avenue and 1st Street.

Hôtel Mirabeau

Hôtel Mirabeau
Lausanne, Switzerland

Yes, well, as I said before, if there's a hotel involved, then there must be women involved. And this hotel is no different. How it became the hotel it is is truly a fascinating story especially when one considers how ugly Mirabeau actually was.

At the age of three, he contracted a horrible case of smallpox that left his face terribly disfigured. Disfigured face or not, Mirabeau led a rather randy life and in 1775 he met Marie Thérèse de Monnier, the famous Sophie of his letters.

Like Valmont, Mirabeau took advantage of a good situation in that after being introduced Mme de Monnier he did whatever he could do to make her fall in love with him. The affair ended by his escaping to Lausanne where Sophie joined him. The hotel, which eventually became the Mirabeau, was their secret hiding place. Though they lived hand to mouth, they had enjoyed the sexual fruits of their flight from their pedestrian lives even though, at the same time, Mirabeau had been condemned to death in absentia for *rapt et vol* (aka abduction and flight). Feeling as if he were part of "France's Most Wanted," Mirabeau tried to avoid capture, but in May, 1777 he was seized by French police and imprisoned in the castle of Vincennes.

Now we know prison means different things for different people and sexual abstinence is one of them. Well, for most people who are imprisoned. At any rate, as a kind of sublimation, Mirabeau began to write the notoriously pornographic *L'Erotica Biblion* which was based on his unfettered fantasies with Sophie. *L'Erotica Biblion* was Mirabeau's answer to incarceration of his sexual energies and in it there were chapters devoted to sexual technique. In a way, it was the *Kama Sutra for French Inmates*. For example, there was advice for how a woman should stroke a man's penis: "The girl . . . should occupy herself only with creating, exciting, and maintaining a plateau of pleasure . . . and then make every effort to suspend sensation at that level, and to delay accelerating it, or even worse, to provoking climax. All her caresses should be calibrated with infinitely delicate nuance . . . Imagine the two actors naked in an alcove surrounded by mirrors and on a bed tilted on an angle. At first, the adept young woman takes the greatest care not to touch the man's genitals; her approaches are slow, her embraces gentle, her kisses more tender than lascivious, her tongue strokes are measured, her glance voluptuous, the intertwining with his limbs full of grace and gentleness; she uses her hands to excite a light tingling on the tips of his nipples; once she perceives that his 'eye' is moist, and she feels that his erection is quite solid, then she gently puts her thumb on the tip of the head of the penis which she finds bathed in lymphatic liquid; from the tip, the thumb gently descends to the root, returns, re-descends, makes a tour of the crown; then the stops, if she perceives that the sensations are building too fast. She then uses only light general caresses, and it is only after the simultaneous and immediate touches of first one hand, then both, and the approach of her entire body, it is only then, just then once the erection has become too violent that she judges that it's the instant to let nature act its course or help it along. That's because the orgasm that is building in the man is becoming so lively and his hair-trigger craving so intense that he would faint away if someone doesn't bring on the grande finale." You get the idea.

With his release from prison, he discovered that Sophie wasn't the woman he thought she was and soon he began a liaison with Mme de Nehra, the daughter of Zwier van Haren, a Dutch statesman and political writer. Now Mme de Nehra was a very sophisticated woman and a woman of a far higher type than Sophie, but the problem for Mirabeau was simple, he needed to finish his erotic masterpiece and the only place he could do it was where it all began in Lausanne. To make a short history shorter, he did, in fact, return to Lausanne with Mme de Nehra and their dog, Chico, where he finally completed *L'Erotica Biblion.* Ironically, the work rendered him impotent and he finally removed himself from the hotel and settled in Pleurer-le-St. Cyclope where he died in 1791. At his death, the hotel, which was previously known as the Hôtel Couillonner, was renamed the Mirabeau in his honor. Should you decide to visit the hotel, ask for room 469. It was, of course, the room in which Mirabeau finished his masterpiece and, by all accounts, inspires those who sleep there with the spirit of *l'erotic biblion.*

Hotel Neruda

Hotel Neruda
Santiago, Chile

To say Neruda was, well, randy would be an understatement. The poet loved women. Lots of women. And his sexual exploits were famous. Almost as famous as his *20 Poemas de amor*. I mean any poet who titles his poetry with titles such as: *Cuerpo de Mujer* (*Body of a Woman*) or *Para mi Corazón* (somehow painfully translated as, *Your Breast is Enough*) or *Niña Morena y Ágil* (also painfully translated as, *Girl Lithe and Tawny*) has a whole lot more on his mind than how to pay the mortgages on three homes. Best to let Neruda describe his relationship with Josie Bliss whom he met in Rangoon: "Sweet Josie Bliss gradually became so brooding and possessive that her jealous tantrums turned into an illness. Except for this, perhaps I would have stayed at her side forever. I loved her naked feet, the white flowers brightening her dark hair. But her temper drove her to savage paroxysms . . . Sometimes a light would wake me up, a ghost moving on the other side of the mosquito net. It was she, dressed in white, brandishing her long, sharpened native knife. It was she, walking around and around my bed for hours at a time, without quite making her mind up to kill me."[25] Experience enough

---

25 *Memoirs*. Pablo Neruda. Translated from the Spanish by Hardie St. Martin. New York: FSG, 1977, p. 87.

---

to end his paroxysmal (and oxymoronic) affair with the "Burmese panther."

In 1930, he met and married María Antonieta Hagenaar, "a Dutch girl with a few drops of Malay blood—and I became very fond of her. She was a tall, gentle girl and knew nothing of the world of arts and letters."[26] Hagenaar knew no Spanish and Neruda knew no Dutch, but knowing Dutch women the way Neruda knew Dutch women knowing Spanish was not very important.

Between 1936-39, she lived with Neruda in Madrid and after moving to Paris they published the journal *Los Poetas del Mundo Defiende al Pueblo Español*. Unlike María Antonieta Hagenaar, Cunard was treated very lovingly in Neruda's memoirs, yet there was never the slightest allusion to being sexually involved with her. But moving on. Curiously, Neruda says very little about his wife, the Argentine painter, Delia del Carril. Neruda and Delia del Carril married in 1943, but the marriage was not recognized in Chile; they separated in 1955.

Neruda married the Chilean singer, Matilde Urrutia, in 1966 and she takes up most of the romantic pages in his memoirs. She was the inspiration of much of Neruda's later poetry, among others *One Hundred Love Sonnets* (1960), but as much as Pablo loved Matilde, Pablo also loved loving women.

Only recently has a book been published that details the sexual appetites of Neruda in a way never detailed before. The book outlines some 200 extramarital affairs that Neruda had over his lifetime, most of which took place in Santiago. Suffering from Casanova's Complex,[27] Neruda was overwhelmed with a libido that

---

26 *Memoirs*, 109.

27 *The Casanova Complex: Neruda, Machu Picchu and other Erections.* Samuel Malone. Boston: Harvart Press, 2001.

he could not control. Though he had a home in Isla Negra, another in Valparaíso, and a third in Santiago, he felt none of them were safe enough for him use for his sexual assignations. At a loss as to what to do, he confided in a close friend, Miguel Huevon, who suggested he use some of his royalty money to buy into a hotel that he could use they way Chilean politicians used the Hotel Valdivia. Neruda thought the idea painfully wise and found a small hotel located at Ave. Pedro de Valdivia 164 in Providencia which he used only for his sexual assignations. At the time, the hotel was called The Hotel Nica Gando, but almost thirty years after Neruda's death, the hotel was leveled and a new one was built in his honor with his name. The hotel description runs thusly:

At the foot of the majestic Andes lie the grand thoroughfares and plazas of the Chilean capital, Santiago. In the heart of one of the city's prime business and shopping districts stands the luxurious Hotel Neruda. From the impressive lobby to the elegantly decorated rooms, this is a truly exclusive urban retreat. Plunge into the heated pool or relax in the sauna before enjoying an evening of cocktails in the bar and fine dining in the Cantalao restaurant. With the added allure of fabulous ski slopes and beautiful beaches nearby, the Hotel Neruda is the perfect place to discover the warmth of Chile.

If you ever go to the Neruda Hotel, mention to the conciérge that Huevon sent you and you're bound to get a special discount.

Saltarelli Realty

Saltarelli Real Estate
Tustin, California

The story about Jacopo Saltarelli and his long affair with DaVinci has already been established. After Leonardo's death, Saltarelli remained in Southern California selling real estate throughout Orange County. Though he too died the same year DaVinci died, the agency remains to this day.

Steinbeck Lodge

Steinbeck Lodge
Monterey, California

In order to appreciate fully Steinbeck's desire to open a motel in Monterey, one needs to know just who and what influenced him. This is an example of how truth seems more fictitious than fiction for it was Robert Louis Stevenson's *Travels With a Donkey in the Cevennes*. In his prologue to the book, Stevenson writes to his friend Sidney Colvin:

The journey which this little book is to describe was very agreeable and fortunate for me. After an uncouth beginning, I had the best of luck to the end. But we are all travellers in what John Bunyan calls the wilderness of this world — all, too, travellers with a donkey: and the best that we find in our travels is an honest friend. He is a fortunate voyager who finds many. We travel, indeed, to find them. They are the end and the reward of life. They keep us worthy of ourselves; and when we are alone, we are only nearer to the absent.

Every book is, in an intimate sense, a circular letter to the friends of him who writes it. They alone take his meaning; they find private messages, assurances of love, and expressions of gratitude, dropped for them in every corner. The public is but a generous patron who defrays the postage. Yet through the letter is directed to all, we have an old and kindly

custom of addressing it on the outside to one. Of what shall a man be proud, if he is not proud of his friends? And so, my dear Sidney Colvin, it is with pride that I sign myself affectionately yours,
R. L. S. VELAY

That book and the advice of Steinbeck's friends (not the least of which was Adlai Stevenson) convinced Steinbeck that a trip through the United States would make for a terrific book. Always ahead of his time, he had a special truck built for him in which Steinbeck could live while on the road. Though he was enthusiastic about his journey through America, his wife was somewhat reluctant to let him go since Steinbeck's health was not the best. He christened his pre-SUV, "Rocinante" in honor of Don Quixote's horse, and with his pet poodle, Charley, embarked on the 10,000 mile journey. Hence the title, *Travels With Charley* after Stevenson's book by a similar title.

Everything was going fine until that fateful evening when Charley came down with a serious case of diarrhea. Clearly, the back of the truck was no place for a diarrhetic poodle, but there was no place for them to go. It was at that point that Steinbeck thought about changing the title from *Travels with Charley, In Search of America* to *Travels with Charley, In Search of a Toilet.*[28] But what did come to Steinbeck's mind was the possibility of starting a motel business that actually catered to animals, specifically dogs, and that was the genesis of the Steinbeck Lodge which opened shortly before his death in 1968 and which remains to this day as an oasis for both man and beast in need of relief at 1300 Munras Avenue, Monterey, CA 93940.

---

28 *Letters from the Great American Road Trip.* John Steinbeck. Pacific Grove, CA: Cannery Row Press, 1963.

Le Stendhal Hôtel

Le Stendhal Hôtel
Paris, France

As mentioned in Stendhal's *Paris*, the opening of the Stendhal Hôtel was the next logical step in the business of making Stendhal financially successful. Once again, it was the countess who encouraged and bankrolled Stendhal in this joint venture. Her ingenious marketing scheme now included the book and the perfume, but, she thought, what would be the next logical step? Sex.[29] But sex where? A hotel, but not just any hotel. With the help of Saltarelli's French connections, they were able to find the exact hotel at the exact location. She fronted Stendhal the money and the two of them initiated the hotel on 31 March 1824.

But the ingenious Stendhal suggested an idea that has now become almost part and parcel of the global marketing business: coupons. It's not entirely clear how Stendhal came up with the idea, but some suggest it was Henry Brulard who gave him the idea. Regardless of who came up with the idea, the idea was an enormous success. They included the discounted coupon with the book and the perfume and the rest is marketing history.

All three businesses were so successful that Stendhal forgot

---

29 *The Green and the Black: Stendhal's Financial Exploits.* Marcel Glouton. Paris: Flammarion, 1995.

about writing again and if it weren't for Fabrizio del Dongo who discovered his work 50 years after his death, the world of letters would only have very little indeed to remember him by. If you go to the hotel, now operated by Julian Sorel, complimentary copies of *L'Amour* are given for every one-night stand and chocolates, wrapped in ribbon that says "Love has always been the most important business in my life, I should say the only one," are left atop every silken pillow.

ROOM <u>SAVER COUPON</u>

EURO
20 OFF
RACK
RTE
7/25 thru
11/30
1-4 per room

Le Hôtel Stendhal *****
22 rue D Casanova
Paris,
FR, *75002
1-800-359-7234

20 Rooms and Suites Hotel Located in the Heart of Paris, a Short Stroll from Vendôme Square, near the Opera House and the Tuileries Gardens. The Hotel Features a Bar and Breakfast Buffet.

of businesses miscellaneous

Apollinaris Water™

Apollinaris Water™
Paris, France

Apollinaire was born Wilhelm-Apollinaris de Kostrowitzky and, as we'll see, the relationship between he and water was not a serendipitous one since who can forget Apollinaire's famous and most masterful poem *L'eau,* a poem so meaningful to him that he not only included it in *Alcools (1913),* but also included an ideographic version in *Calligrammes (1918)* which was only recently discovered. It was one of his most moving and passionate poems and within it lay the seeds for what would be his most successful business venture. This idea was alluded to in a letter the teenage Apollinaire sent to Mallarmé in 1898 only months before Mallarmé died. In it, Apollinaire wrote to Mallarmé regarding the latter's obsession with water and suggested, naively, that he and Mallarmé go into business together selling water. Of course, Mallarmé wrote it off as mere adolescent playfulness and never responded. But one only needs to look through the pages of *Calligrames* to detect Apollinaire's obsession. The poems in *Calligrames* are filled with allusions to water: *Lettre-Océan, Il Pleut, La Colombe Poignardée et le Jet d'Eau, Océan de Terre,* his moving, *Le Chant d'Eau, L'Eau dans les Oreilles,* and *Chant de L'Eau en Champagne* all of which come from the *Calligrames.* But it was also well known that Apollinaire was somewhat intrigued by the occult, by prophecies and dreams. One such dream was both prescient and prophetic.

In a recent book on Apollinaire, *Death and Water*,[30] the author, René Rimbaud, writes of a particular dream Apollinaire had in August, 1918. Rimbaud alludes to the pandemic influenza that took place between 1918-1919 and which killed more people than World War I. Known as the "Spanish Flu" or "La Grippe," it was considered the most lethal epidemic in human history killing between 20-40 million people. With that context in mind, one can see how prescient Apollinaire's dream actually was.

According to Rimbaud, Apollinaire, who had a fascination with the apocalypse even as a child, had a dream in which the figure of Death was plowing the French fields of Champagne turning over body upon body. In the background, placards read "la grippe." At some point, Death stopped and reached for a bottle of water the label on which read, "Apollinaris." Apollinaire immediately awoke and wrote the dream down in his journal. The journal entry was dated 2 August 1918.[31] Death and Champagne were only natural as Apollinaire fought on the front lines in Champagne and witnessed first hand the death of comrades and enemies alike. The relationship of "la grippe" to Apollinaire was a bit more disconcerting. In subsequent entries, Apollinaire wrote vividly of the death and destruction the influenza had caused and how the medical community was incapable of stopping the disease. He too felt himself susceptible to the disease and wrote such, but he recalled the dream and the water and it was at that time that he and his fiancée, Jacqueline Kolb, decided that, perhaps, it was the

---

30 *La Mort et L'Eau.* René Rimbaud translated by Raymond Federman. Paris: Flammarion, 2003.

31 *The Influenza Journals.* Andrew Sars. New York: Misbegotten Press, 2003.

water that might help. With that in mind, they took it upon themselves to begin producing water high in calcium, magnesium, sodium, potassium in hopes that the combination might prove effective against the plague.

Arranging an agreement with a German bottler, on 31 October 1918, the first bottle of Apollinaire's Apollinaris water was sold to mixed reviews. Some found it marvelous, others found it heavy. Regardless of what others thought, based on his dream, Apollinaire was absolutely convinced the mineral content of the water would, in fact, retard the virus and he consumed several liters a day. Unfortunately, a day later, 1 November 1918, Apollinaire himself contracted "la grippe" and on 9 November he died from it. But the last words he spoke were extremely important and, given the SARS epidemic, prescient. "Qu'est-ce que ça fout?"

Though in fact the water did not cure nor prevent disease, it did hydrate. Eventually, the company was sold to the Kreuzberg family and is now one of the biggest producers of mineral water in Germany.

Aceites Borges™

Aceites Borges™
Tàrrega, Spain

Of course with the success of the travel agency (See: *Borges' Travel, Hemingway's Garage*) Borges couldn't stand still and he was eager to explore other avenues of investment. But just where the suggestion for olive oil came from was beyond belief. It's no secret that Borges' political leanings were to the right of right. He often lauded Peron as a "gentlemen," lunched with General Jorge Videla, allegedly dedicated the first copy of his translation of "Leaves of Grass" to Richard Nixon, and praised Pinochet as being a "leader." In 1973, when Peronists were elected, Borges called it a "government of scoundrels." In 1975, he was quoted as saying: "When I think of the cases of torture [in Argentina] I have the impression that my country is disintegrating morally as well as economically." In March, 1976, when informed that Evita had lost, Borges wept and when he met Videla, he thanked him for "having liberated the country from the infamy which we bore." Only Elvis could have been any farther to the right.

So it was only natural that in 1976, at the age of 77, he would receive la Gran Cruz de la Orden al Mérito Bernardo O'Higgins from none other than the Chilean dictator, Augusto Pinochet. Borges was thrilled. Or as thrilled as anyone could be by meeting a dictator.

Borges wanted to go to Chile and receive the award on behalf of his Chilean readers. Unfortunately, at the same time, the Nobel Prize committee was deciding whether to give the award to Borges or not and advised him that a trip to Chile might not be in his best interest. Not only did he go, but to make matters worse he had his picture taken with Pinochet who, sitting cross-legged in his suit and tie looked every bit as regal as a dictator could possibly look.

The award ceremony over, Pinochet had Borges feted with a dinner and during the dinner the two of them talked of different things[32] not the least of which was Borges' travel agency which Pinochet said he would use the next time he left the country.[33] During the course of their meal, Pinochet opined that one couldn't really find a good olive oil for salad. He asked Borges if he felt the same way. Borges allegedly agreed and for the next hour Borges talked non-stop about olive oils. It was not by accident that Borges knew about olive oils since he spent considerable time in Italy and Spain and in addition to knowing their writers, knew their oils. He waxed poetically about such things as cleaning olives, grinding olives to paste, mixing to increase olive oil yield, separating the oil and water from the olive, separating the oil from the water, processing the oil, storing and bottling the oil, tasting and rating the oil, making flavored oils. Borges was a veritable font of olive oil information; however, Pinochet was decidedly not

---

32 According to Volodia Teitelboim nothing they talked about remotely resembled politics.

33 In fact, this took place when Pinochet decided to visit London in 1998. There were some hard feelings afterwards when the travel agency would not reimburse Pinochet for missing his flight even after Pinochet wrote there were mitigating circumstances that precluded him from leaving. The new head of the agency, Knut Hamsun, wrote back expressing concern, but stated the letter had "disappeared."

interested in olive oil. It was merely a point of conversation since Pinochet had never read anything by Borges and couldn't tell the difference between a circular ruin and a forking path.

To shut Borges up as diplomatically as he was able, Pinochet suggested that with all that knowledge Borges might consider going into the olive oil business. It was an extraordinary suggestion and one that Borges not only took to heart, but commenced. Once when asked if the trip to Chile were worth it, considering it cost him the Nobel Prize, Borges opined, "A good olive oil is the precious life blood of a master spirit." Apparently, some prizes were worth more than others.

Brecht's BMW

Brecht's BMW
Escondido, California

Anyone who knows anything about Brecht's life knows how utterly disappointed Brecht he was by failing to make the big bucks as a screenwriter in Hollywood, but what everyone doesn't know is how he finally managed to make a living while he lived there. The truth is truly stranger than fiction.

Brecht arrived in Hollywood in 1941, with the help of his good friend, Lion Feuchtwanger. But while Feuchtwanger was raking in a lot of Hollywood dough, Brecht was raking banana leaves. As a matter of fact, he was so anguished by his failure in Hollywood that he was once quoted as saying "Jeden Morgen, mein Brot zu verdienen, Gehe ich auf den Markt, wo Lügen gekauft werden. Hoffnungsvoll, Reihe ich mich ein zwischen die Verkäufer." In English it doesn't sound much better, "Every morning, to earn my bread, I go to the market where lies are bought. Full of hope, I line up among the salesmen." Welcome to Hollywood.

Eventually, Brecht rented a house on 26th Street in Santa Monica about which he wrote, " . . . [it was] one of the oldest, is about 30 years old, California clapboard, whitewashed, with an upper floor with 4 bedrooms. I have a long workroom (almost seven meters), which we immediately whitewashed and equipped with four tables.

There are old trees in the garden (a pepper tree and a fig tree). Rent is \$60 per month. \$12.50 more than in 25ᵗʰ Street." Meanwhile, in Pacific Palisades, Feuchtwanger was living in the 'Villa Aurora' which even by today's standards is considered opulent. The disparity grated on Brecht who couldn't reconcile how Hollywood valorized the mediocre and relegated intellect to penury.

During his first year in Hollywood, Brecht came up with a number of ideas for screenplays and wrote a number of scripts, including "Joe Fleischhacker," a collaboration with screenwriter, Ferdinand Reyher. Brecht also worked with Fritz Lang and later with screenwriter, John Wexley. The two of them worked ceaselessly for two months on the final script, but what Brecht discovered 60 years ago works much the same way today. That is, most of what he wrote was discarded and none of his contributions ever got him a film credit. He discovered that Hollywood was not Berlin and wit and intellect were little match in a market that was predicated on glitz. To that end, Eisenstein's words ring true. (See: *Eisenstein's Café*).

Enter Hemingway. By accident, Brecht's car broke down in Santa Ana while on a weekend outing to Laguna Beach. As fate would have it, AAA towed the car to Hemingway's Garage (see *Borges' Travel, Hemingway's Garage*) when Hemingway himself showed up. Coincidentally, Hemingway was also on his way to Laguna Beach to look for property to purchase for a café. While they worked on his car, Hemingway and Brecht had breakfast at DaVinci's Restaurant and after Brecht relieved himself of all that troubled him about being a screenwriter, Hemingway suggested that he "Fuck Hollywood and the screenwriters" since "they're all Jews anyway." He went on to say, "You can make some decent dough selling BMW's in Southern California and if you play your cards right, get laid in the process."[34]

Brecht didn't think much about the idea since he was practically broke, but Hemingway said he'd help bankroll the business. So the oddest couple of all,[35] Hemingway and Brecht, opened Brecht BMW in the fall of 1942. Brecht managed the business for several years making enough money to return to Switzerland in 1947 the day after his appearance before the House Un-American Activities Committee on 30 October 1947. Before he left the US, he opined that he was saddened by the fact the HUAC didn't interrogate him on Halloween since "what better day to carry out a witch hunt."[36]

Though he sold his share of the franchise shortly before he left the country, the dealership remains in his name today and can be found in Escondido, California.

---

34 *From Carburetors to Carbohydrates: Hemingway's Orange County Businesses.* I.M. Slavish. Newport Beach, CA: OC Publishing, 2001. *Hemingway was alluding to the wealthy, widowed Orange County women who preferred BMW to Mercedes; however, what Hemingway didn't know then, but was to learn later, was that Brecht "liked to hit from both sides of the plate."*

35 The Hemingway-Brecht relationship was the initial idea behind the Matthau-Lemmon film, *The Odd Couple*, directed by Gene Saks, written by Neil Simon.

36 *Bluster & Bullshit: Brecht's Hollywood Diaries.* Kurt Weill. Boston: Harvart Press, 1949.

Optica Cellini

Optica Cellini
Buenos Aires, Argentina

No mistaking it, Cellini needed to get out of Italy and fast. Probably no other artist, living or dead, (except, perhaps, that scoundrel Villon) needed to find a safe haven away from the personal and legal imbroglios that followed him. But then again, Cellini was his own worst enemy. As you can find on the internet, Cellini was one of those larger-than-life figures of the Italian Renaissance: a celebrated sculptor, goldsmith, author and soldier. But there was also something very different about Cellini that put him in that Villonesque category; you see, Cellini enjoying killing men as much as casting bronze statues.

In a way, Cellini made Charles Manson look like a mere bicycle thief. If one can believe his *Autobiography*, Cellini murdered the Constable of Bourbon and, later, murdered Philibert, Prince of Orange, as well. As a matter of fact, even Pope Paul III was willing to pardon him for an indiscriminate murder carried out on the streets of Rome! In 1529, his brother, Cecchino, who assassinated a constable in Rome and was wounded in the mêlée, died from his wounds. Outraged, Cellini hunted down the man who wounded him and killed him too!

It would seem that Cellini's homicides and acts of indiscriminate violence were condoned by Popes and Princes alike simply because they wanted to avail themselves of the maestro's incredible talents; however, even maestro's can overdo certain things and after an altercation with Pietro Alvise Farnese, the Pope's natural son, he fled to Florence and Venice. But those instances were mere piddlings compared to what really drove Cellini out of Italy and to Argentina. The reason for that can be found in his *Memoirs* concerning one Caterina Micceri.

If I did not confess that in some of these episodes I acted wrongly, the world might think I was not telling the truth about those in which I say I acted rightly. Therefore I admit that it was a mistake to inflict so singular a vengeance upon Pagolo Micceri. . . . Not satisfied with having made him take a vicious drab to wife, I completed my revenge by inviting her to sit to me as a model, and dealing with her thus. I gave her thirty sous a day, paid in advance, and a good meal, and obliged her to pose for me naked. Then I made her serve my pleasure, out of spite against her husband, jeering at them both the while. Furthermore, I kept her for hours together in position, greatly to her discomfort. This gave her as much annoyance as it gave me pleasure; for she was beautifully made, and brought me much credit as a model. At last, noticing that I did not treat her with the same consideration as before her marriage, she began to grumble and talk big in her French way about her husband. . . . the wretch redoubled her insulting speeches, always prating big about her husband, till she goaded me beyond the bounds of reason. Yielding myself up to blind rage, I seized her by the hair, and dragged her up and down my room, beating and kicking her till I was tired. . . . When I had well pounded her she swore that she would never visit me again. Then for the first time I perceived that I had acted very wrongly; for I was losing a grand model, who brought me honour through my art. Moreover, when I saw her body all torn and bruised and swollen, I reflected that, even if I persuaded her to return, I should have to put her under medical treatment for at least a fortnight before I could make use of her. [The next morning Caterina returns.] Afterwards I began to model from her, during which occurred some amorous diversions; and at last, just at the same hour as on the previous day, she irritated me to such a pitch that I gave her the same drubbing. So we went on several days, repeating the old round like clockwork. There was little or no variation in the incidents (344-347).

What happened next was totally unexpected. Not only did Caterina's husband Paogolo put out a restraining order on Cellini, but he also hired a couple of Sicilian thugs to "take care of Cellini." Cellini got wind of the plan from a cousin of Cosimo de'Medici who, not indelicately, told him that if he didn't leave Italy immediately he'd be "deader than Kelsey's nuts." Not having the faintest idea who Kelsey was, Cellini figured de' Medici's cousin knew something he didn't and he immediately left Rome for Naples and took the first ship out, named the Nicagando, which, coincidentally, was headed for the port of Buenos Aires.

Once there, the master, who, under the patronage of Cosimo de' Medici, crafted some of the finest works in metal, including the bronze bust of Cosimo himself and the colossal statue Perseus and Medusa, decided to turn his talents to creating distinctive eyewear for Argentines. And though he kept a fairly low profile in Buenos Aires, it was clear that though you might be able to take Italy out of the murderer you can't take the murderer out of Italy. The rumour was that Cellini did, in fact, have a volatile romantic relationship with the Argentine novelist, Luisa Valenzuela and the male protagonist in her short story, *"The Word 'Killer'"*, in the collection titled, *Cambio de Armas*, was none other than Cellini. Though Valenzuela has neither confirmed nor denied the allegations, the rumours persist to this day. After the rather tumultuous relationship with Valenzuela ended, Cellini decided to return to Florence where he died leaving the optical business to his cousin, Vinny. The store remains in Buenos Aires at Arenales 1736.

Cervantes Seguridad

Cervantes Seguridad
Buenos Aires, Argentina

It all started when Cervantes went to his physician, Cide Hamete Benegeli. According to the journal[37] he began in 1605 shortly after the publication of *Don Quixote*, Cervantes visited his physician with the following symptoms: fatigue, loss of a sense of well being, joint aches and stiffness of hands, hot flashes, sleep disturbances and worst of all, a reduced libido. When he asked his physician what the problem could be the physician laughed and merely said, "Andropause." By that time, Cervantes was 58 and had been separated from his wife Catalina de Salazar y Palacios for nearly 18 years. Needless to say, he was getting a bit long in the tooth and short in other anatomical parts. But deciding on what to do was not going to be easy and he debated on how to approach the problem. In a very un-Cervantean manner, he records in his journal that he began a correspondence with one Alonso Fernandez de Avellaneda,[38] a journalist who wrote a self-help column for men in Madrid's *Diario Medico.* In the letter, Cervantes recounted his symptoms to Avellaneda telling him also, in very direct terms, that

---

37 *Despues el Quixote.* Miguel Cervantes. Edited by Nico Gando. Madrid: Planeta, 2001.

38 *The Cervantes-Avellaneda Letters.* Edited by Nico Gando. Madrid: Planeta, 2003.

"Hace mucho tiempo que no tengo una pichada." Avellaneda immediately responded by telling Cervantes that the symptoms were all too obvious for someone his age and what he needed to do was change his career. Cervantes wrote back asking what Avellaneda had in mind and the latter responded with two words: security systems. Cervantes responded, asking why security systems to which Avellaneda responded that security systems would be the wave of the future and predicted that there would be a global need for security in the future. As more and more countries turned to a neo-Liberal economy and more and more people became less concerned with their humanity and more concerned with their purchases, there would indeed be a need for security systems to be put in place. But, he added, it all depended on the marketing those systems and the best way to market anything was with the use of what Avellaneda called, "papaya." Cervantes got the idea. Avellaneda actually suggested places to go for funding of such a business including the Madrid Small Business Association. Filled with a renewed enthusiasm, Cervantes decided to embark on the project simultaneous with his writing of *Don Quixote Part II.* What Cervantes didn't know was that Avellaneda had his own plan.

The truth was that Alonso Fernandez de Avellaneda was a pen name used by an unknown Spanish writer who published a spurious second part of *Don Quixote* in 1614, a year before Cervantes's own second part appeared (1615). Avellaneda was fully aware of who Cervantes was and while the latter was busily engaged in building a new start-up company, Avellaneda was busy writing *Don Quixote Part II* in an attempt to cash in on the original. It was the ultimate of ironies in that Cervantes was trying to work on a security systems business while, at the same time, the security of his life's work was being undermined.

Needless to say, the entire scam dis-spirited Cervantes and his health deteriorated quickly resulting in his death in 1616. Almost four centuries later, Avellenada's true identity has been established. In a remarkable book written by Ricardo Ejevarilla,[39] Avellenada has been unmasked as no one other than Lope de Vega who outlived Cervantes by almost another twenty years. For those of you who are interested, the woman soliciting customers for Cervantes is none other than a distant relative of La Chirinos, a character from Cervantes' mini-play, *The Marvelous Pageant.*

---

39 *The Secret History of Lope de Vegvellenada.* Ricardo Ejevarilla. Madrid: Planeta, 2003.

Faulkner's Mower Shop

Faulkner's Mower Shop
Costa Mesa, California

There's the story about Faulkner and Clark Gable riding together in a limo. Gable asks Faulkner what books he's written. Faulkner pauses then responds with, what films have you made. That was before he got fired from MGM. So what else would a down-home boy like Faulkner do in order to make a living at least for the short term? And though Faulkner was never very fond of living in Southern California, movies were in his blood. If Faulkner took some of California back to Mississippi, he brought a lot of Mississippi to California. And since he wasn't making a whole lot of money from his fiction and since Faulkner couldn't be far from his Hollywood agent, Shorty Lazar, he decided to go into the lawnmower repair business as a way of staying financially afloat. How he got there is a bit of Hollywood history itself.

Faulkner, of course, had the reputation of being the fastest scriptwriter in Hollywood. That reputation was based on the fact that Howard Hawks asked Faulkner to come up with the script for *Today We Live* which he did it in five days! Allegedly, Stallone said he wrote *Rocky* in five days, but, well, I'm not even going to say it. At any rate, things weren't going that well for Faulkner and after he was fired from MGM he had to move out of the Highland Hotel in

Hollywood to something less costly. His good friend, Nathanael West, apparently had some contacts in Costa Mesa and Faulkner reluctantly headed south.

West's friend, Balso Snell, worked with horses and had a small bungalow in Costa Mesa out of which he ran an equestrian school. Faulkner, who rode horses (but not very well), was trying to figure out what he could do to keep himself occupied while waiting for another big call from Hollywood. The idea came to him as he watched Snell mowing his lawn one June morning. Snell was a daydreamer. Always dreaming of a better life or a different life and so he was dreaming about ancient Greece when he happened to roll over a stone so huge that it lodged in the blades. Faulkner came to Snell's rescue and as he was trying to fix the mower asked Snell if there were anyone in the area who actually repaired lawnmowers. Snell thought about it for a moment and said no. Hence, the birth of an idea and the birth of Faulkner's Lawnmower Repair.

Of course, Faulkner didn't remain in Costa Mesa nor did he remain in Hollywood, a city, he wrote, "of almost incalculable wealth whose queerly appropriate fate it is to be erected upon a few spools of a substance whose value is computed in billions and which may be completely destroyed in that second's instant of a careless match between the moment of striking and the moment when the strike might have sprung and stamped it out." However, Faulkner did make sojourns back to the Golden State strictly for the cash and though he sold the business to Lemuel Pitken, those halcyon days of repairing mowers found their way into many of his works including such classics as: *As I Stand Mowing, Grass Burning, A Blade of Grass for Emily, Go Down, Mower* not to mention *Mowing in August.* He received the Nobel Prize for Literature in 1950 and at Howard Hawks' request, he made one more trip to Hollywood in February 1951 to rework the script *"The Left Hand of God"* for 20th Century-Fox.

Ironically, a fall from a horse likely contributed to his death and as he was helped from the ground he was quoted as saying, "I should have stuck to lawnmowers."

Gautier Furniture

Gautier Furniture
Le Boupère, France

Of course, what would a man with Gautier's aesthetics actually do? A novelist, a poet, a critic and painter, the man who turned the phrase "art for art's sake" into a household phrase that aesthetic beauty was the sole purpose of a work of art. But like most of his Symbolist friends, pre-Symbolist friends, post-Symbolist friends or even non-Symbolist friends, he too was often light on cash.

Gautier, like his dear friend, Nerval, as always strapped financially. Unlike Nerval, Gautier at least had some success as a journalist. Unfortunately, he was never elected to the Académie Française, and his government appointments and subsidies were never sufficient. More than once did he ask for a post as Inspecteur des Beaux-Arts and more than once was he denied. To make matters worse, he was involved in a lawsuit in which a certain François Buloz alleged that Gautier owed him 2300 francs as an advance for some novel that went unwritten. Gautier was bailed out by his patron saint, Mirès, a Marseilles banker, who had the money wired to Paris in order to "Get Gautier out of Buloz' claws." But Mirès' help lasted only a short time and soon enough Gautier was back in the clutches of financial despond. He once wrote to his aging sisters that "All my regret is that I'm not richer and that I give you so little. I am responsible for you to our dear father and mother, now dead, and while I am alive you will always have what I've not needed to promise you . . . Imagine having to write copy when your mid is racked by all these anxieties; imagine having to be gracious, entertaining and gay with a crowd of people, and you can judge if I spend my time pleasantly! You know how disgusted and bored I am with men and things; I live only for those I love, for, personally, I have no pleasure left on earth."[40] On his 48th birthday he was to write, "On that unfortunate date I entered the world where I was to write so much ill-paid and useless copy."[41] Something had to be done. Flaubert had sent a letter to George Sand stating that he thought Gautier was dying of "ennui and misery." Just when things couldn't get any worse, enter the *deus ex machina.*

It just so happened that Musset, who had made a lot of money with his perfume, was looking for a hedge against inflation. He heard of Gautier's plight through Sand and felt obligated to help. Perhaps it had something to do with what Gautier wrote about Musset's work in 1842 in which the former said, "M. de Musset has written a whole book of comedies and proverbs, full of the most twinkling spangles of fantasy and the sweetest tears of sensibility."[42] It so happened, that Musset's uncle, who lived in Le Boupère, wanted to get out of the furniture business. Musset said it would be a great opportunity for Gautier and allow him a semblance of financial security he had never had while affording

40 *Théophile Gautier: His Life and Times.* Joanna Richardson. London: Max
  Reinhardt, 1958, p. 159.
41 Ibid, p. 162.
42 Ibid. p. 70-71

him time to devote to his work.

At first, Gautier thought Musset's idea "C'est vraiment la merde!" But Musset said that with Gautier's aesthetic sense and with what Saint-Beuve called his innovative sense of art, he would be able to run the store admirably. All of his friends, from Balzac to Zola agreed that a change in climate and a change in business would lessen his anxieties and contribute a few more years to his life. And so in October, 1870, Gautier became the CEO of the furniture store that now bears his name.

Grieg Seafood

Grieg Seafood™
Bergen, Norway

Grieg was, arguably, the finest Norwegian composer of the late 19th century. His work was extraordinarily diverse. Collaborating with playwrights like Bjørnson for the play *Sigurd Jorsalfar* and with Ibsen in *Peer Gynt*, Grieg showed how multi-talented he was. And though he composed both orchestral and chamber music he wrote an enormous amount of material for the piano.

As anyone knows, or should, the sea plays an immense role in the lives of all Norwegians and Grieg was not immune to that kind of maritime infection. One merely needs to look at the titles of some of his compositions: *Siren's Enticement, Six Norwegian Seascapes, I went fishing so late, The Entry of the Fishermen, Dance of the Sea King's Daughter, Two Nordic Fishing Melodies* among others to realize that, sooner or later, the sea would play a major role in his life. Just what sort of role was to be seen.

In 1874, Grieg was awarded a Norwegian state artists' grant which enabled him to compose without recourse to teaching in order to make money. For years he had tried, albeit unsuccessfully, to garner an NEA grant for composition, but the Endowment always told him, politely that his work was not "cutting edge" enough so the grant was a godsend for him. Unfortunately, not all went well. He returned to his native Bergen, but fell victim to states of depression. Being a period of pre-Prozac, Grieg had to fight the depression the only way he could: through his music. Unfortunately, too, the money began to run out and he had to take conducting posts and from 1880-1882 he conducted the Harmonien Orchestra of Bergen, but soon thereafter he resigned that post as well.

What happened after 1885 were a series of extraordinary events that altered the course of his life. Always in dire financial straits, in 1885 Grieg moved into his new home "Troldhaugen," outside Bergen where he lived out the rest of his life. But a very serendipitous moment occurred in 1900 a very young Maurice Ravel was visiting Oslo and had the opportunity to meet the maestro. Ravel is quoted as saying to Grieg, "The generation of French composers to which I belong has been strongly attracted to your music. There is no composer to whom I feel a closer affinity—besides Debussy—than you." Of course, Grieg was flattered, but Ravel also detected something else about Grieg: his concern about his retirement. His concern was that he would not be able to maintain Troldhaugen and the fear of his home being repossessed haunted him. Ravel, who had already started his shoe business (See: *Borges' Travel, Hemingway's Garage*) suggested to the maestro that he invest in some business that would garner him a safe and secure future. Ravel even suggested that he would lend him some "start-up" money.[43] During the course of his meeting with Grieg, Ravel asked him what he would do if he had the opportunity to start up a business. Grieg didn't hesitate at all: fishing. The two of them

---

43 *Memories of the Maestro: Ravel's Notes on Edvard Grieg.* Oslo: Grieg Publishing, 2004.

discussed what could be done and on 31 March 1902, Grieg inaugurated his business: Grieg Seafood which specialized in fish farming and processing.

The company was a huge success and garnered Grieg all the money he needed for the rest of his life. Thrilled as he was about the success of the fish farm he even wrote a piece of music titled, The Salmon Maid, a cycle of 8 songs, Op.67. Until his death, Grieg devoted his attention both to his music and to his seafood business and when he died in 1907 the company was taken over by one of Grieg's nephews who passed on the company to its present day owners who have relocated their headquarters at Grieg Gaarden in Bergen. As their website states: "Today Grieg Seafood commands all aspects of salmon and cod farming, from production of brood stock and eggs to the final filets and steaks and most delicious smoked and marinated seafood." Nothing would have pleased the maestro more.

Lautréamont Bookstore

Lautréamont Bookstore
Santiago, Chile

It's common knowledge that Comte de Lautréamont was not Comte de Lautréamont, but Isidore Lucien Ducasse. What is uncommon knowledge is that Isidore Lucien Ducasse was not French, but Uruguayan and what's even more uncommon knowledge is that he was Jewish.

Isidore Lucien Ducasse wrote under the name Comte de Lautréamont, a *nom de plume* he stole from the Eugene Sue character, Lautréaumont and though Ducasse admired the French and French writers, he never felt quite at home in Paris and often thought about how to return to South America. First published in 1869, *Les Chants de Maldoror* deals with the ghoulish character, Maldoror, part Fantômas (before Fantômas, 1911) part Dracula (before Dracula, 1897) whose nefarious deeds included torture, homicide, sado-eroticism, and, worst of all, unmitigated urges to become a literary agent. What people tend to ignore is that Ducasse was Jewish and was well-versed in Jewish folklore. One can see elements of the Golem legend creeping into *Maldoror* as one could see elements of the *Golem of Prague* in Ducasse himself. Ducasse has been described by those who knew him as silent, withdrawn, pale, hippy-ish with a deep and profound admiration for Poe, Baudelaire,

Sade, Dumas, Maturin and all those other "creepy guys"[44] like Catulle Mendès, Jean Richepin, Charles Nodier and Petrus Borel.

According to some, while working on *Les Chants de Maldoror*, Lautréamont would sit for hours writing at his piano while simultaneously banging out atonal rhythms on the keyboard a technique Schoenberg was to use in his own compositions in 1908 only after reading Ducasse's book. But his death was even odder than his life. He died a year after publication of the book at the age of 24 in one of the most mysterious of all deaths ever recorded in France. Allegedly, he was found dead in a hotel room located at 7, Faubourg-Montmarte. On his death certificate the cause of death was listed as "unknown" which is about as strange a death to die from as one can possibly imagine. What has been proven is that Ducasse never died, but actually staged his death precisely to get back to South America!

The proof comes from a book written by Ducasse's great-nephew, Isidore Ducasse, in his biography titled *Tio Maldoror*.[45] In that biography, Ducasse states that his great-uncle Ducasse had a number of fetishes and sexual fantasies and got himself into a lot of debt from buying sex toys, erotic aids and pornographic books. The only money he had was his Bar Mitzvah money which he could not spend except for a dire emergency.

So, Ducasse had a dilemma He wanted to return to South America, but had little money to do so. According to Ducasse, Ducasse knew someone in the Paris police department who owed him a favor. Apparently, this particular officer, Inspector Narish,

---

44 *Récit Qui Donne La Chair De Poule*. Barbey Huysmans. Paris: Edition Rampant, 1999.

45 *Tio Maldoror: The Short, Sad Life of Lautréamont*. Isidore Ducasse. Mosquito Press, Santiago, Chile, 2003.

frequented a particular brothel that Ducasse knew well. One night they ran into each other. Narish, concerned about appearances (which was odd for a Parisian policeman), asked Ducasse to keep it quiet which Ducasse did. But when Ducasse wanted to get back to South America he came up with the idea of faking his death and having Narish take care of "the body." Narish thought it wise to do so since he'd be rid of Ducasse and Ducasse would be rid of Paris.

The plan was arranged thusly. Ducasse would take a prescribed dosage of Belladonna that would mimic a state of mortality. Narish would show up at a particular time, declare him dead of "unknown"

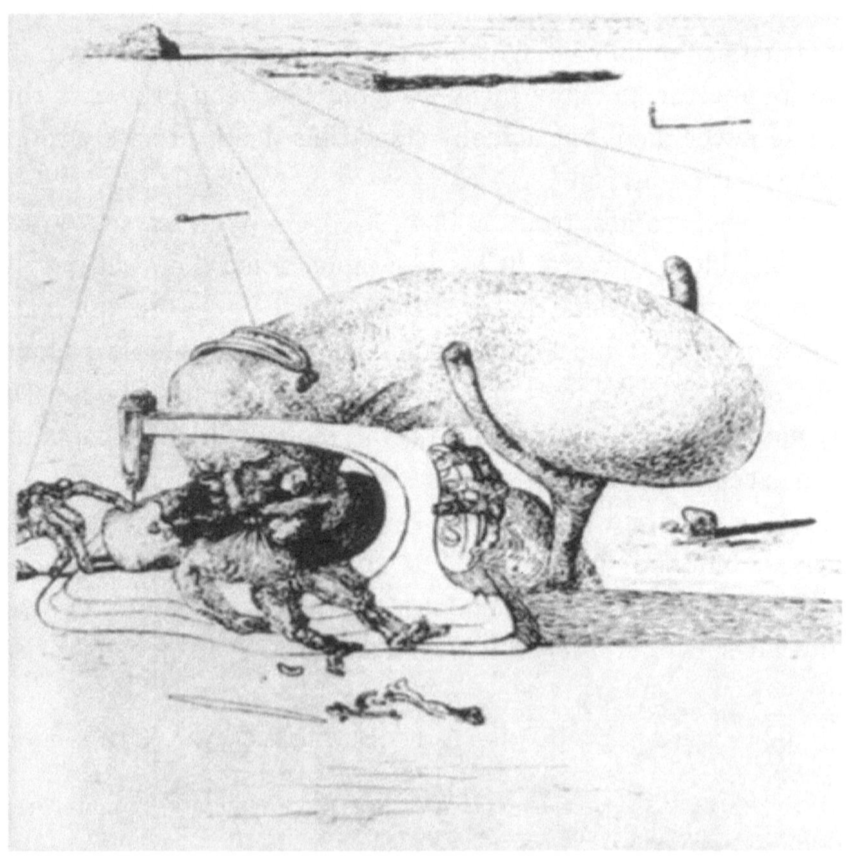

causes and have the body shipped back to Uruguay. The plan worked marvelously. Narish sneaked him aboard the next ship to Uruguay, but Narish, who didn't speak any Spanish, accidentally put him on board a ship headed to Chile instead of Uruguay. When he got to the port of Valparaíso, Ducasse realized he didn't have enough money to return to Montevideo. He remembered his cousins in Santiago and went to visit them. They were enormously pleased to see him and took him out to dinner in Bellavista. After having dinner, Ducasse chanced upon a store for lease. Trying to make the best out of a bad situation, he decided to do something he had always wanted to do. Namely, open a bookstore. Instead of returning to Montevideo, he remained in Santiago and the bookstore, located in Bellavista, not only remains to this day, but also houses the heretofore never recovered drawing by Dalí.

Magritte Leathers

Magritte Leathers
Buenos Aires, Argentina

Magritte once wrote, "Last night and today I have been reading some Borges that Georgette gave me. My first impression hasn't changed. It's a kind of mind I don't like. I admit he 'mixes up' a lot of ideas I don't 'get' at all. He mixes like loquacious and ineffectual speakers who aren't totally ineffectual, since they produce unbearable boredom. I don't mind his creating illusion, his bluffing, or his posting as an 'honest man,' but in spite of all the sham brilliance of his discourse, I consider Borges to be an educated prick."

With that kind of attitude, you can imagine how incomprehensible it would have been for the two of them to have become linked in business, but, in fact, that's what happened. Magritte was always fascinated by women. Nude women. Surreal women. Parts of women. Just a glance at his *oeuvre* would attest to that . . . *Il ne parle pas*, "*L'évidence éternelle, L'univers mental, La magie noire, La ligne de vie, La liberté de l'esprit, La philoophie dans le boudoir, Olympia, Lola de Valence, Le galet, L'Âge du plaisir, Les liaisons dangereuses.*" So the thought of opening a leather good store only for women wasn't as outrageous an idea as it might at first sound. A leather store owned by Borges would.

Magritte traveled extensively. Europe, the Middle East, the United States, South America. It was on one of those South American sojourns that Magritte fell in love with Buenos Aires and the tango. So much so that he envisioned an entire series of paintings of nudes merely titled, "Tango."[46] One afternoon, he and his wife Georgette were walking along Florida looking for a leather wallet. They came upon a store that sold the most marvelous leather goods for women that Magritte was so overwhelmed with the place he actually made inquiries into whether the store were for sale. By a curious coincidence, it was. The owner, Bustos Domecq was planning to leave Argentina for California in order to open another business (See: *Borges' Travel, Hemingway's Garage*) and was actually looking for someone to buy his. It seemed like the perfect business opportunity for Magritte and the papers were drawn and signed. It was only after the papers were signed that Magritte discovered the person who owned the property was none other than Borges and so in a story that was even too Borgesian to have been written by Borges and too Magrittean to have been painted by Magritte, Borges became Magritte's landlord![47]

The thought of paying rent to the "educated prick" was even too surreal for Magritte and so he eventually sold the business back to Domecq who, by that time, had gone into partnership with Bioy Casares. At any rate, Magritte's still exists on Florida selling some of the finest leather goods in Buenos Aires.

---

46 The series was never started, but the idea for doing so was taken on by the Argentine-Chilean painter, Camilo Ambrosio.

47 In yet another irony of ironies, in 2003 El Centro Cultural Borges put on an exhibit of 61 photographs taken by Magritte between 1925-1955. It was one of the most well-attended exhibits in the history of the Centro Cultural Borges.

Milton's Baking Company™

Milton's Baking Company™ *Del Mar, California*

What Brueghel could do, Milton thought he could do better. So the question remains: how does one go from *Paradise Lost* to Del Mar? It's one of the most intriguing bits of literary/entrepreneurial business that one can possibly imagine. It all begins with Milton's Cambridge days when he attended Christ's College. He had entered Cambridge with the idea that he would enter the ministry; however, he was expelled from Cambridge for a term after a fistfight with one of his tutors. The reason? It seems his tutor, one Francois Bibelot, said that compared with French bread, English bread was "merde." Initially, no one could understand why Milton took the statement so personally, though one of his classmates suggested that Milton's uncle was a bread baker and Milton felt an insult to English bread baking was an insult to his uncle and, by extension, to himself.

The connection between Milton and bread baking was borne out when, during his expulsion, he gave up studying for the ministry and spent six years working part-time for his bread baking uncle and writing during which time he wrote: *L'ALLEGRO, IL PENSEROSO* (1632), *COMUS* (1634), and *LYCIDAS* (1637). Towards the end of the decade, he traveled to France and Italy where he met Galileo who was blind at the time. Milton's conversations with Galileo were recorded in his *AREOPAGITICA*, which attacked censorship. The irony, of course, was that Milton too would become blind, but not before he learned the craft of baking.

By the mid-1640s, Milton began to have vision problems. The exact cause of Milton's blindness is not exactly known; however, it has been reduced to two: glaucoma and AMD, age related macular degeneration. Because Milton was fairly young when he was completely blind, the latter has been ruled out and so we think the cause of his blindness was due to an early onset of glaucoma. Whatever the cause, Milton was blind at the age of 43. What's of interest here is not the cause of his blindness, but what he learned to do as he was losing his sight.

Coterminous with writing *Paradise Lost,* Milton returned to his uncle's bakery fearful that when he went blind completely he'd have no adequate source of income. His marriage with Mary Powell was in the tank (though he'd have two more "tankful" marriages) and he knew he'd need a trade to "put bread on the table." His uncle, with the curious name of Milton Milton, suggested he take up bread baking and taught him everything he needed to know. Milton became so adept at the baker's art that he could knead the bread with his eyes closed. This was, in fact, the whole point. When he left his uncles' bakery he could go through every baking procedure without seeing what he was doing.

Milton returned to Chalfont, St. Giles, Buckinghamshire where he opened his own bakery, Milton's Bakery Company, and in between writing *Paradise Lost* and baking scones and such, he also had time for two more marriages, both of which only validated what he wrote in *THE DOCTRINE AND DISCIPLINE OF DIVORCE* (1643). At any rate, Milton died from 'gout struck in' on November 8, 1674 and was buried beside his father in St Giles', Cripplegate. Curiously, it wasn't until 1998 that his *Brief History of Baking* (circa 1671) was discovered beneath a loose tile in the kitchen of Milton's house. An extraordinary find, I here include one of the maestro's favorite recipes which he called Milton's Mélange:

Take fayre Flowre and the whyte of Eyroun and the yolk, a lytel. Then take Warme Berme, and putte al thes to-gederys and bete hem to-gederys with thin hond tyl it be schort and thikke y-now, and cast Sugre y-now ther-to, and thenne let rest a whyle. An kaste in a fayre place in the oven and late bake y-now. And then with a knyfe cutte yt round a-bove in maner of a crowne, and kepe the crust that thou kyttest, and then cate ther-in clarifiyd Boter and Mille the cromes and the botere to-gederes, and kevere it a-yen with the cruste that thou kyttest a-way. Than putte it in the oven ayen a lytil tyme and then take it out, and serve it forth.

The bakery eventually disappeared, but the fame of Milton's baked goods lingered on and the name was eventually trademarked by two Jewish entrepreneurs in California who, fascinated with Milton's story, "re-opened" the bakery in Del Mar. And the cycle of history closes since one of their specialties is Healthy Multi-Grain English Muffins. That's English muffin, not French.

Musil's Muslix™

Musil's Muslix™
Vienna, Austria

According to most biographers, Robert Musil was not very pleasant company. Some believe the reason for his irritability was due to a spastic colon and Swiss medical records tend to validate that assumption. Some believe it was the disease that contributed to the creation of *muslix*. Others suggest it was chronic poverty.

Adolf Frise indexed, in his *Plädoyer für Robert Musil* (1982), the qualities that were associated with Robert Musil by those who knew him consisted of being: proud, uncommunicative, cold, critical, elegant, polite, well dressed, aloof, dismissive. He was all those things and more, but most of these qualities have been associated with two other aspects. The poverty he had to deal with for the greater part of his life, and his attitude towards other authors of his time. Both come, biographers often state, from his earnestly felt lack of recognition as an important figure in German letters.

In 1911, Musil married and published two novellas about women, *Die Vollendung Der Liebe* and *Die Versunchuing Der Stillen Veronika*, under the title *Vereinigungen* which only exacerbated his fragile financial situation since Musil was always in dire need of money: always wondering how he and his wife Martha would live through the next day. In his diary, there are regularly complaints that they only have little money left to live on. Between 1911 and 1914, Musil took odd jobs in an attempt to survive: a Viennese librarian; a stint with the Austrian army during WWI; a stint as a civil servant with the Defence Ministry after WWI. When government terminated Musil's job, he became a full-time writer and freelance journalist in the 1920s.

He did achieve some short-lived success in the 20's, but his condition rapidly deteriorated when he began his one great masterpiece, *The Man Without Qualities* and the combination of little money and enormous stress not only contributed to increased intestinal disorders, but, eventually, a mental breakdown in 1929. However, it was in 1927 that a most unlikely meeting took place. Musil's doctor informed him that he would have to go on a high fiber, low carbohydrate diet for the rest of his life if he were going to live productively and he recommended a health resort in Bad Herrenalb in the Black Forest. It was at that time Musil ran into none other than Herman Hesse who himself was recuperating. The two got into a conversation[48] not only about their writing, but also about their individual complaints and that's when the idea arose.

Hesse began work on *Siddhartha* in 1919 and it was published three years later. Hesse told Musil it was the culmination of his immersion in Eastern philosophy and spirituality not to mention Eastern diets and one of the items he mentioned to Musil was a cereal that would, he said, "cleanse the fabric of your soul."[49] It was called *Anaah*. Musil asked Hesse what was in it and Hesse told him it was a gluten-free mixed cereal about a third of which contained

---

48 *From Siddhartha to Muslix: The Hesse-Musil Correspondence.* Jean-Paul Novalis. Berlin: Weltschmerz Verlag, 1952.
49 Ibid.

dried fruits, nuts and seeds. Musil wanted to know more and asked what were the ingredients to which Hesse told him dried soya flakes, sugar beet fibre, corn flakes coated with honey, rice flakes, dried pieces of apricots, dates, figs, apples, raisins, coarse of soya, sunflower seeds, soya grains, banana chips, and linseed. Musil asked him where he could buy such a cereal, but to that question, Hesse merely shrugged his shoulders and said, Talatscheri, India. Obviously, Musil was disappointed, but he did have the ingredients and an idea.

Returning to Berlin, where he lived until 1933, Musil didn't think very seriously about the project until moving to Vienna. He continued struggling with his novel while his financial situation began to get worse and worse. Finally, in 1937, while doodling on a napkin[50] at the Kaffeehäuser Frauenhuber writing variations of his own name, he accidentally inserted an "X" an came up with the name—M U S L I X. The name stuck. He copyrighted the name, and with some financial backing from Hesse began to manufacture the cereal in March, 1938. As Musil's luck would have it, a week later Hitler invaded Vienna and Musil and his wife had to flee Vienna and abandon the business. It was too much for Musil and he only four years later he died in Geneva impoverished and in relative obscurity.

But even in death, Musil suffered financially. After the allies liberated Vienna, a copy of the contract between Hesse and Musil was found in the latter's apartment along with some abandoned manuscripts and a copy of the ingredients. No one knows exactly how the recipe found its way from Vienna to Battle Creek or how the name got changed from Muslix to Mueslix, but today the

---

50 This napkin is included in a major art project called the *Projet Serviette* funded by the National Endowment for the Humanities.

Kellogg Company owns the copyright and offers a choice of Harvest Feast Mueslix, Almond Raison Mueslix, Banana Nut Mueslix and Apple Crisp Mueslix all for $4.89 a box. Musil gets no residuals.

Vermeer Manufacturing™

Vermeer Manufacturing™
Pella, Iowa

It was only a matter of time before Vermeer got tired of living the provincial life in Delft. Granted he considered himself a kind of an entrepreneur of sorts, but trying to raise a family of eleven children on the income of a painter, especially of a painter who was as meticulously slow as Vermeer, was have been impossible. He dabbled as an art dealer in order to make some extra cash, but disaster struck in 1672 when much of Holland was occupied by the French and the general economic crisis forced Vermeer to lease his own house and move in with his mother-in-law. What happened in that house on the Oude Langedijk.

Living in Delft, Vermeer never tired of countryside and many of his paintings reflected that love of nature. One only needs to look at such paintings as *Chirst in the Garden of Mary and Martha* (1654-65) or *Diana and Her Companions in the Forest* (1654) or *The Little Street Next to the Pond* (1658) to see that there was a connection between Vermeer and the environment. That connection to the environment was never more pronounced than in his painting *View of Delft* (1661) and the suggestion his mother-in-law made to Vermeer based on the painting. According to a letter dated 14 February 1672 from Vermeer to Johannes van der Meer, the man who rented Vermeer's house, Vermeer alluded to the possibility of going into the business of manufacturing machines to be used for environmental purposes and wanted van der Meer to be a partner. The idea, suggested to Vermeer by his mother-in-law and based on what she perceived to be a lack of erosion control *vis-à-vis* the painting, prompted Vermeer to think seriously about connecting his interest in the environment with making money at it. It was true that there were absolutely no businesses at the time devoted to such things as erosion control.

The idea was clearly "cutting edge" and van der Meer, who was a keen businessman himself, met with Vermeer at the Stadscafe De Wang to discuss the possibility of such an enterprise. Finally, he thought, he found a way out of financial turmoil and a way to provide for his family. Van der Meer was extremely keen on the idea and the company began to make erosion control machines that not only increased job performance, but decreased mulching time and labor. The business was an extraordinary success and enabled Vermeer to spend less time painting and more time contracting clients. Ironically, Vermeer's success with the company is what contributed to his very small *oeuvre* which most experts agree did not exceed three dozen pieces.

Unfortunately, Vermeer did not live long enough to enjoy the fruits of that initial labor and on 15 December 1675, only three years after he started the business, he died leaving eight children behind. He was only 43. Van der Meer was distraught by Vermeer's death and felt he could no longer operate the company effectively in Holland. Fortunately, Van der Meer's cousin knew someone who worked for Saltarelli Realty. The agent suggested that Van der Meer consider moving his company to Fontana, California which was, at the time, soliciting businesses to move there by granted major tax breaks. Flushed with the idea of moving to "the new world," Van der Meer left Delft with his family and moved to Fontana where the company still exists and as an homage to his friend and partner has kept the name Vermeer, a name synonymous with Brush Chippers, Stump Cutters, and Tree Spades.

Valenzuela Azul
Buenos Aires, Argentina

Let's face it, it's not the business Valenzuela wanted to get into, but it's hers nonetheless. Originally, she wanted to open a store called *Valenzuela for Men*. Lord only knows what she would have done with that place. Presumably, it was going to be a clothing store, but not everyone was so certain about her intentions. Oh sure, she comes off as a feminist, but with titles like *Bedside Manners* and the sexually charged, *"City of the Unknown"* (written when she was a teen) not to mention the fact that she was married at 20, and moved to Paris where she could have been influenced by those *Nouveau Roman* women writers (that would include people like Duras and Sarraute) one begins to wonder that a moving company was merely a front for something else. Something much more nefarious. One might have thought that the moving company was merely a moving company to "move" men from wherever they were into some secret confines that Valenzuela had. Something akin to *Bluebeard's Castle*. I shivered at the thought, but then I discovered the truth.

Actually, I know this first-hand after overhearing a conversation she had in the restaurant Chiquilin (Sarmiento and Corrientes; the *bife de chorizo* is to die for) while I was visiting Buenos Aires. Who knows how these things happen, but I was having dinner with a painter friend of mine, the brilliant painter, Alejandro Boim, when who should walk in but Valenzuela and the Argentine painter, Carlos Muslera. I only knew it was Muslera because Boim told me, but I had heard about Muslera from the Chilean painter, Camilo Ambrosio. At any rate, the two of them sat down at a table next to ours and I could overhear their entire conversation about how she wanted a clothing store, but it wasn't going to happen so she was going to invest some money in a moving company. When Muslera asked her why a moving company she said, "To move men, what else." I was shocked! What I had anticipated was true. He had plans to kidnap men, move them in her moving vans and do who knows what to them.

To validate the fact that I was there and heard these things, I interrupted their dinner conversation and politely asked: "Are you Luisa Valenzuela?" She said, yes. I said, "I'm a great admirer of your work, do you think I could get a photo of me with you and Carlos?" They agreed and here it is.

It certainly was very kind of them to take a photograph with me and we actually had an enjoyable evening talking about her decision to invest in a moving company when her first inclination was a clothing store for men. Valenzuela was very forthright in saying that if she "couldn't get them into a pair of pants then she'd have the pants get into them." I wasn't sure about what that actually meant and, perhaps, I missed something in my translation, but be that as it may she was the person responsible for doing the hiring so whatever she wanted, she got. And that included me. That night she asked me if I'd like to join her for breakfast at her home the next day. I agreed, but reluctantly since I still wasn't quite sure where her moving company was actually a moving company or a moving company.

At breakfast, we were talking about writing (or was it the existential question: Why do agents exist?) and I asked, *au passant*, an ironic passing, if she had prepared the breakfast for me. She gave me what I heard was one of her patented Valenzuela gazes. A *Valenzuela gaze* (not to be confused with a *Lacanian gaze*) is something that peaks out from the corner of her eyes (not exactly a sidelong glance since it is a gaze, mind you, and sidelong glances are usually found in Balzac novels) which bespoke of what she would soon say which was something to the effect that if you remember anything about me, remember I don't spend a lot of time in the kitchen. Or something to that effect. Perhaps, it wasn't exactly those words, but the meaning was clear. I certainly wasn't going to look a lizard's tale in the mouth nor was I going to complain to Clara about some lack of symmetries even though strange things must have happened here, there, especially in terms of bedside, or, tableside, manners. Don't censor me.

Breakfast concluded we adjourned to her study and continued our chat. I felt secure in knowing that the moving company was just that: a moving company and not a conveyance for the kidnapping of men. So, if you're ever in need of a moving company in Buenos Aires, remember to call Valenzuela Azul: she will move you whether you want to be moved or not.

Axelrod Dairy™

Axelrod Dairy™
Binghamton, NY

"**B**uy why yogurt?" was the question Axelrod's wife asked him when the former decided to give up the toy store in La Jolla. "And why New York? La Jolla is the best climate in the world!" To answer those questions, one must return to Axelrod's childhood and the influence that calcium had on him.

As everyone knows, calcium deficiency can cause a lot of physical problems. Low calcium levels can produce painful muscle contractions with dizziness, confusion, and even seizures and that lack of calcium seems to affect the upper right cerebral cortex resulting in some rather extraordinary behavior. It is common knowledge that, for a number of years, Axelrod had such a calcium deficiency which his family physician, Dr. Robert Mouser, diagnosed as *chronic calciumania*. This chronic calciumania led Axelrod to the production of a number of literary texts that were not only convoluted, but also totally incomprehensible for most of his readers. Even his brother had given up reading them. "I tried," he said, "but I didn't understand a freakin' thing." Among those works were his novels, *Cardboard Castles; Cloud Castles; Capital Castles; The Posthumous Memoirs of Blase Kubash;* the Secret Histories, *Borges' Travel, Hemingway's Garage* and the pages you're reading now,

Balzac's Coffee, DaVinci's Ristorante and a potpourri of pusillanimous prose not yet perpetrated on the American public.

It was becoming too much for Axelrod . . . the satire, irony, litotes . . . and he felt the only way to get back to "normal" and begin writing the kind of fiction that would be popular and sell was to "get calcium" and the best way to get calcium was to buy a dairy. At the time, his then-wife thought that a bit extreme, but he refused to budge. "A day without calcium," he was wont to say, "is like a day without a realistic plot," and, so, with little delay he sold his toy store in La Jolla (See: *Borges' Travel, Hemingway's Garage*), fled the bitter tranquility of Southern California for the bitter frigidity of upper New York and bought himself a dairy.

Today, Axelrod lives a sedentary life in Binghamton with his wife, son, and hundreds of dairy cattle. Yet there are those moments when the long and chronic years of calciumania reappear and when that happens it's anyone's guess as to what he might write.

ABOUT THE AUTHOR

MARK AXELROD is a Professor of Comparative Literature in the Department of English at Chapman University, Orange, California and for twenty years has been the Director of the John Fowles Center for Creative Writing. He has won a number of awards including Fulbrights and NEA grants and has published extensively in fiction, non-fiction, film and literary criticism. His latest Black Scat book was the short story collection, *Dante's Foil & Other Sporting Tales* and the translation of Balzac's play, *Mercadet,* which was re-titled *Waiting for Godeau.* He recently finished a novel titled, *The Mad Diary of Malcolm Malarkey* that is being considered for film production under the title, *Malarkey,* starring Malcolm McDowell.